THE FLAME'S BURDEN

MATTHEW KARABACHE

ISBN 13: 978-0-9924470-3-8 (Paperback edition)
ISBN 13: 978-0-9924470-4-5 (Kindle edition)
ISBN 13: 978-0-9924470-5-2 (PDF edition)

www.matthewkarabache.com
www.facebook.com/matthew.karabache

Houngan Igul stopped, raising a varicose-veined hand to signal for the men behind him to do the same. Ask obeyed the silent instruction, adjusting his grip on the haft of his spear as he glanced to either side. The leaf-stripped birch of the forest seemed to press in on them. The old, dirt-encrusted snow beneath his feet crunched softly as he shifted his weight from one foot to the other.

The houngan turned, his ice-blue eyes scanning the trees for a few moments before he opened his mouth. 'It is near,' he said quietly. 'Spread out. Do not lose sight of each other.'

The Innsmen fanned out, shooting each other anxious glances as they searched through the trees. Ask strained his ears to hear over the sound of his heart pounding in his chest. His breathing quickened, painting the air in front of him with small plumes of quickly dissipating white mist. Looking to his left, he caught Fulnir's eye. His lanky friend gave him a lopsided grin that was meant to be encouraging, but failed to mask its wearer's unease.

A sharp yell rent the air. Every muscle in Ask's body tensed. He spun around, locating the source of the cry and breaking into a sprint towards it. Though he covered the two dozen yards in a scant handful of seconds, it was too late.

Blood stained the white of the snow in an angry, comet-shaped blotch. At its centre was Grein. The bulky warrior seemed to be leaning against a tree, as though he was only resting for a moment. As Ask drew closer, however, he could see that the man's throat had been viciously torn out. Strands of ragged flesh hung from the gaping wound, dripping red.

Houngan Igul and the others quickly converged on his position, coming to stand in a rough semi-circle around the

1

body of their fallen comrade. Ask looked over at them and shook his head. 'It moved too swiftly. He had no time to defend himself.'

Bergr nervously touched the pendant that hung at his throat, the anxious gesture odd on a man of his size, and looked toward Igul. 'What manner of *monskellr* are we hunting, houngan, that it is able to steal up on us without warning?'

'I am still unsure,' Igul said, frowning. 'We must be cautious until I am able to determine how it may be stopped and destroyed. Leave him for now. We will return for the body once we have ended this.'

Haering snarled in frustration, a guttural sound from deep in his throat. He stalked up to the corpse, bending down to retrieve Grein's fallen axe. Hefting the fallen warrior's weapon, Haering scowled darkly. 'His axe will taste the blood of his killer before the day is done. This I swear.'

Scanning the trees around them, Igul paused for a moment to consider their next move before indicating a path through the forest with a pointed finger. 'We divide into two groups. Ask, with me. The rest of you stay close to each other.'

A murmur of 'yes, houngan' rippled through the group.

Ask and Igul traced the trailing tail of the bloody pink-red comet that stained the snow. A dozen yards on, they'd lost sight of the second group of warriors.

Ask tried to focus his mind on sensing the creature's presence, but gave up in exasperation after a minute or two in favour of his more mundane senses. He had never been overly skilled at detecting spiritual energies. With his teacher standing right next to him it felt like his efforts were woefully redundant. It would be better for him to keep his eyes and ears alert to any hint of movement that might betray the creature they hunted. They walked in silence as several minutes crawled past.

The hair at the back of Ask's neck prickled. Something heavy crashed into him from behind, slamming him to the ground. His skull cracked against the raised root of a tree as he went down. His limbs went slack, his spear falling from nerveless fingers. A dank, foetid breath rasped near his ear. White lines of pain erupted along his back as something raked his flesh, slicing through the layers of leather and furs he wore as though they weren't even there.

A heavy pressure on his shoulder blades ground him into the snow. Ask waited helplessly for the killing blow, but the pressure pinning him vanished. Surprised, he rolled over in time to catch a glimpse of some sort of hazy distortion moving through the air, hurtling towards Houngan Igul. The old man had his staff up, lips moving, though through the ringing in his ears Ask could hear no words. A flash of white and gold blinded him. For a moment he could see nothing. Bracing against the ground with the heel of his hand, Ask pushed himself up into a sitting position, blinking away the black and purple spots clouding his vision.

He could have only missed a second or two, but somehow Igul had covered the ground between them and was now standing right over him. A stream of crimson traced a cobweb pattern down the left side of Ask's teacher's face from a gash on his temple; a twisted reflection of the black whorls of the tattoos across his other cheek. His ironwood staff was held lightly in one hand in a loose defensive posture and his asson, his ceremonial rattle, was held firmly in the other.

'*Kald Sann Seithsdóttir, mwen bezwen bon konprann ou.*'

The fragments of stone and bone within his asson thrummed with power as Igul shook it rhythmically and chanted words in the Old Tongue. His eyes were locked unwaveringly on something just past where Ask sat.

Reaching out with his free hand, Ask felt about for his spear, eyes following the houngan's gaze. There was something there, several yards away. He could see the disturbed snow torn up where it had landed hard on the ground. There was a faint shimmer in the air, like a heat haze, but the form was completely indistinct.

'*Revele sa ki kache yo epi yo montre sa a verite a!*'

Igul's voice thundered to a crescendo as he finished the evocation. The creature abruptly came into focus, the magic obscuring it from view dropping off like a cloak.

It had no eyes. Where the creature's eyes should be were only two black hollows, ringed with scar tissue, as though they had been torn out long ago. It was a long-limbed, hairless thing, man-sized, with a hunched back and dark green, bruise-like skin. Its arms and legs rippled with thick muscles and ended in inches-long claws. Long fangs hung from its lipless mouth.

Behind him, Ask heard Igul say one word, low and quiet: 'Tokoloshe.'

The beast opened its mouth and roared—a deep, inhuman sound that scratched at Ask's eardrums and sent a jolt of primitive fear through his hindbrain. It lunged towards them.

Ask's fingers closed around the familiar wood of his spear and he brought it up reflexively. White fire shot through his back as he moved, but he pushed the pain to the back of his mind. Too slowly, Ask pushed himself forward to stand and meet the creature's attack. Beside him, Igul was smashed to the ground. Ask turned and thrust awkwardly with his spear. The iron head of his weapon scraped against the creature's side, but did not find purchase.

The tokoloshe shrieked as it scrabbled at Igul, the houngan struggling to block its claws with the gnarled wood of his staff. Ask yanked his spear back and steadied himself for a half-second before firmly taking the haft in both hands and stabbing forward, aiming for the creature's armpit. The head struck home and Ask leaned in, pushing as hard as he could. The iron bit deeply into the green-black flesh and dark, greasy blood spurted from the wound. The tokoloshe recoiled, hissing in pain and anger. Igul took advantage of the motion, heaving at his staff to push the creature further off balance and shove its bulk off of him. It rolled away, howling as Ask's weapon ripped free.

Ask took one hand off his spear to reach down and grab at Igul, pulling the houngan to his feet. The tokoloshe hesitated for a moment, then turned and bounded off into the trees, loping on all fours like a wolf.

Houngan Igul slapped Ask's hand away and pointed after the retreating form. 'Do not let it escape! If it finds water to drink it will be able to conceal its form again!'

Ask nodded and broke into a run after the creature. It was much faster than him, but wounded. His only chance of catching it would be if its injury forced it to stop to rest.

Ask ran, hurtling through the trees as fast as his legs would carry him, eyes locked on his quarry. He stumbled once or twice, scattering half-melted snow as he kicked through it. A fallen branch almost tripped him. When he looked up, the creature had vanished, but the trail it had left was still clear as day. He sprinted on. The muscles in his legs burned as he pushed himself harder, his lungs demanding more air than he could breathe in.

The trail ended abruptly and he stumbled to a stop. Whipping his head around, he looked for a sign that would indicate the direction the tokoloshe had fled. There was a mound of slushy snow where it looked like the creature had skidded to a stop next to a jagged, lightning-blasted tree stump. A splatter of grey blood tainted the already dirty white snow, but the ground showed no further sign of the creature.

Ask looked up, craning his neck to peer into the bare branches above.

The *monskellr* dropped on him from the tree with a guttural roar of fury. Ask raised his spear, impaling the creature as it slammed him into the ground, driving the air from his lungs. The wounds on his back exploded into a bout of fresh pain and his vision was suddenly clouded by tears.

The tokoloshe shrieked in pain and pulled back. Ask heard the haft of his spear splinter as the weapon was wrenched from his grasp and suddenly he could breathe again. He tried to pull himself up, but only succeeded in struggling up onto one knee.

The tokoloshe was less than three feet away from him, half of his spear sunk deep in its ribcage. Its face contorted as it snarled and spat, clawing at the splintered wood puncturing its breast. Grey blood oozed out onto the snow. Ask could see that the beast was trembling slightly, though whether from pain or exhaustion or fear he did not know. Fixing its eyeless gaze upon him, the tokoloshe snarled again. It raised one claw high in the air, ready to cut the life from him.

Ask raised his own hand in a feeble mirror of the gesture. *'Lesir Hyrr bondye, pwoteje sèvitè ou kont sa ki mal sa a!'* he shouted desperately.

There was a clang, like metal striking metal, a sizzle of flesh and the tokoloshe yelped like a kicked dog.

Ask opened his eyes. His hand was holding steady in front of him, just touching the inside edge of a barely visible, heat-like haze that enveloped him. Beyond the sphere, the tokoloshe had retreated a few paces, nursing a burnt, blackened hand. For a few moments, there was no sound save for the heavy rasping of its breath.

A wave of relief surged up through Ask's chest. The protective barrier would have posed no obstacle at all to a human foe, but the energy he had mustered would be enough to keep out a malignant spirit like the tokoloshe. Ask concentrated on the spiritual haze he had erected, pouring whatever energy he could muster into it. With another word of the Old Tongue, he pushed the barrier outward, increasing the sphere's diameter by a foot or two. Ask faltered, instantly regretting the action as he felt the energy start to slip away. He grasped the shield desperately, clinging to it with the last scraps of his willpower. The tokoloshe snorted and shied away from him, then turned to lope off.

'For Grein!' Haering charged out from between two trees. He brought Grein's axe down in a heavy overhand chop, catching his target in the neck. His other hand stabbed up under the creature's ribcage with his spear. The ferocity of the attack knocked the tokoloshe from its feet. Its feeble shriek of pain was cut short as Haering hefted the axe and brought it down a second time. Ask lay still, safe within his spiritual barrier, as Haering hacked at the creature a few more times to ensure it was dead.

A moment or two later, Fulnir and Bergr appeared cautiously through the trees. The two of them couldn't look more different, Ask noted. Fulnir lanky and sandy-blond, Bergr enormous and black-haired.

'Ask!' said Fulnir, relief tinging his voice. 'Virding smiles upon you.'

After only a moment's pause, Igul's second hounsis stepped unimpeded through the shimmering haze of Ask's barrier and offered his hand. 'I worried that the creature had ended you as well.'

Exhausted, Ask let his hand fall limply to the ground. Around them, the barrier faded away into nothingness. He could barely think. Every time his heart beat, it felt like someone was striking him in the head with a hammer.

'I was fortunate. It was a near thing. Too near,' he managed to say.

With an effort, he managed to reach out and gratefully took his friend's forearm. Fulnir hauled him to his feet and clapped him on the back. A fresh wave of pain exploded across Ask's body and he stumbled forward. He would have fallen if the other apprentice hadn't caught him.

'Kerling's teats! Are you wounded? I did not realise...' Fulnir said. There was concern in his friend's voice. His gloved fingers were sticky with Ask's blood.

'I will live,' Ask said, grimacing.

'Here, let me take a look.'

Fulnir stepped around to get a better look at Ask's back. There was a stab of pain as his fingers probed and pulled aside the cut and torn furs, but Ask managed to remain relatively still. He heard his friend suck in air through his teeth.

'How bad is it?'

'You are lucky that you spent some time lying in the snow. I think that is all that has kept you from bleeding out,' Fulnir said. 'We need to bind your wounds. You are going to have some impressive-looking scars. I almost envy you.'

Ask was starting to feel light-headed. 'I doubt you would say that that if you knew how much this hurts. I think it broke a few of my ribs as well.' He swayed slightly as he spoke. Fulnir's grip was the only thing keeping him on his feet.

'I did say 'almost'.'

Fulnir carefully peeled the furs from Ask's back, using a sharp knife to cut at the seams. A stab of pain lanced through Ask's body at every movement. He bowed his head and tried to focus on his breathing instead; deeply in, then out. Fulnir's movements were quick and precise. Igul had taught them both how to clean and care for wounds and Fulnir had shown an especial aptitude for it.

Snow crunched somewhere to Ask's right. 'Is he well?' Haering asked, a touch of anxiousness in his tone.

'I will be fine,' Ask murmured, before Fulnir had a chance to respond. 'You do not need to worry about me so much.'

The older man snorted. 'I raised you, I can worry when I damn well please.'

Another set of footsteps in the snow. Ask tentatively cast out his senses and felt the comforting presence of Houngan Igul. He continued past Ask. The young apprentice pictured the houngan in his mind, walking over to the corpse of the tokoloshe to inspect it. He could hear his master's voice, though he could not make out the words. It sounded like a chant; likely an invocation to the Lesir over the tokoloshe's corpse to ensure it was dead and would remain so.

Ask started to shiver, though he could not tell if it was from the loss of blood or the cold. Fulnir covered his wounds and put pressure on them, tying the crude bandages in place with strips of leather. Ask listed to one side, his body feeling as though it would start to float away, and almost fell over again. This time, Igul was the one to steady him. Ask opened his eyes and reached up to cover his master's hand with his own, using the contact to anchor his mind from falling into unconsciousness.

'I felt your invocation,' said Igul. 'An impressive amount of power, but sloppy. What did you do?'

'There was some sort of haze around him when I got here. I could see it, but it did not do anything to me.' Fulnir's voice came from somewhere behind Ask.

'A barrier?' Igul's tone was thoughtful. 'I would have thought that beyond your strength. Unfocused, though, otherwise it would not have been visible and I would not have felt your energy slopping out everywhere. You overexerted yourself. No wonder you can barely stand. It surprises me that you are conscious at all.' A glimmer of a smile ghosted across his wrinkled face.

Ask nodded mutely, too exhausted and light-headed to respond, then grimaced as the throbbing pain in his skull intensified. Igul was right, he had put too much of himself into it. He'd be lucky if he didn't spend the next few days nursing a headache and a sick stomach.

'You have accomplished much this day, my hounsis. You still have much to learn, but there is little left that I am able to teach you. The day after tomorrow is the last day of winter. It will be an auspicious evening to hold the raising ceremony. Two days hence, you will be a houngan.'

Igul's words were completely unexpected and hit Ask harder than anything the tokoloshe had managed. 'Thank you, houngan,' he managed to say.

He could scarcely believe it. His apprenticeship was to be completed. His teacher was ready to initiate him into the deeper mysteries of the Lesir and acknowledge him as an equal.

Houngan Igul shushed him. 'Save your strength, you'll need it to get back to the village.'

The old man turned to the man standing beside him. 'On our return, inform Erlend that I require a runner sent to Houngan Hafgrim. He will wish to attend Ask's initiation.'

Haering nodded briskly. 'Yes, houngan.' He moved to help Fulnir support Ask's weight.

Before they left, Ask looked back toward the grey-splattered snow where the tokoloshe's body lay. Haering had done a thorough job of butchering the creature. There was a faintly acrid odour in the air that Ask could smell even from here. It looked as though the green-black flesh was starting to melt and slough off its bones. Ask could see a light dusting of a yellowish powder over the corpse. Sulfur; likely part of the ritual Igul had performed to ensure that the spirit would never return.

Once Houngan Igul consulted the sky and breeze to determine which direction would return them to Innset, he took the lead and strode off into the forest. Trembling, Ask leaned heavily on the two men supporting him, letting them take most of his weight. Together, they followed the houngan as quickly as his injuries would allow them to. Despite the pain, Ask felt a glowing sense of pride and satisfaction. Two days. Two days and he would be a houngan.

- - -

Brilliant tongues of red and orange leapt from the bonfire, adding wild splashes of colour to the starkly contrasted black of the sky and dirty white of the melting snow. Houngan Igul reached into the base of the fire and scooped up a handful of black ash, seemingly untouched by the intense heat. He added it to the plate of cornmeal he held in his other hand and stirred the mixture with a finger as he walked back towards the patch of earth that had been cleared for the ceremony.

Ask knelt at the edge of the circle, a white scarf still tied around his head from the purification ritual that Igul had performed with him earlier that afternoon. The injuries he had sustained the other day still ached. The stitches that Igul had sewn into the wounds in his back especially so, but his head had finally ceased throbbing. His excitement at what was to come had pushed the remaining pain to the back of his mind. After seven long years of training, he was finally ready to become a houngan in his own right. It was slightly disheartening that Houngan Hafgrim had not appeared for the ceremony, but Ask's disappointment was quickly swept aside by anticipation of what was to come.

Beside him, Fulnir busied himself checking the goat that Erlend, Innset's headsman, had given them for the evening's work. He glanced over at Ask for a moment, shooting him an excited grin from under his mane of shaggy blond hair. As Houngan Igul's other apprentice, Fulnir would also play an important part in the ritual this evening.

The animal watched the proceedings dispassionately, masticating a tough patch of grass that had managed to survive the winter. Actually sacrificing a goat like this was something reserved for only the most important of rites.

The three drummers across the clearing—Haering, Eydis, and Eydis' daughter Isond—took up their instruments and began to beat out a rhythmic cadence to signal the beginning of the ceremony. The villagers drew close in hushed excitement.

Pouring the mixture of cornmeal and ash between his fingers, Houngan Igul stepped through the precise, measured motions required to create Kald Jarl Løgur's runic veve on the patch of cleared ground. He moved in time to the beating of the drums, turning the ritual into a dance as he traced the familiar pattern across the earth. Despite his age, he moved smoothly, fluidly, as the symbol took shape beneath him.

As the last of the cornmeal spilled onto the ground, Ask rose to his feet and joined the houngan, careful not to disturb the freshly-laid lines just yet.

'Jarl Løgur, tanpri ouvri nan pòtay lavil la. Mwen prezante w ak yon ofrann epi mande pou benediksyon ou!'

Words of the Old Tongue spilled from Igul's lips. He brought forth his asson and shook it. The sharp rattle of the fragments of bone and stone inside joining with the beat of the drums as Haering and the others increased the tempo of their music.

The drums spoke of the Jarl as well. Haering and Eydis beat out a loud, strong cadence that Isond responded to with a lighter, almost jaunty counterpoint. The beat intensified, louder and faster, and Ask grinned as he felt the energy Igul had gathered pass through him. Turning slowly on his heel to face Fulnir, he let out a loud whoop of exultation, exploding into a flurry of movement. The stitches on his back should have burst open at the sudden shock. Ask should have collapsed to the ground from pain as his injuries protested against the dance. The energy of the ritual, however, filled him to the brim and overrode his body's objections, leaving him free to jump and twirl.

Fulnir raised his own voice in answer to Ask's cry and leapt in to join them. The three men danced together wildly, recklessly. Ask could feel the energy flow out and charge the space as their feet scattered the cornmeal symbol and ground it into the earth.

Ask felt his heart surge. He spun and weaved and jumped, his vision blurred by streaks of multi-coloured light. His lungs burned, but he let out another yell of delight as he was caught up in the intensity of the energy they were channelling. He knew that the dance only lasted scant minutes, but to him it felt like hours. All of his excitement, all of the anticipation that had been building up over the past few days, came spilling out as he danced and twisted almost frantically, losing track of everything around him.

When Jarl Løgur arrived, however, he felt it. The air around them felt as though it had frozen solid. Ask let it bring him to a sudden stop. Around them, the Innsmen and drummers fell silent. Ask looked around for Igul and Fulnir to see which one of them had been mounted. Igul was next to him, breathing hard. The old man's ragged grey hair and beard were a complete mess, but otherwise he looked normal. Turning to look behind him, Ask dropped his eyes to see Fulnir writhing on the ground.

Ask and Igul stepped back, giving the convulsing man plenty of room. Within seconds, Fulnir was pulling himself back to his feet as though nothing had happened. Except, of course, it was no longer Fulnir. His posture was different, shoulders back in an exaggerated display of confidence, a jaunty grin painted across his features.

Houngan Igul stepped forward and inclined his head respectfully. *'Byenveni, Kald Jarl Løgur.'*

'Li la bon fè isit la, houngan!' The spirit inhabiting Fulnir spoke with a loud, booming voice that didn't match the skinny body it was coming from. The jarl smiled widely, the expression odd on Fulnir's features. 'It is a good night tonight. I can feel the cold deep in my bones.'

Even as the houngan greeted the spirit, Ask was already moving towards the edge of the circle, heading for the goat that Bergr held steady on the outskirts. The large man saw him coming and knelt down next to the animal. He whispered reassuringly into its ear and put one arm around its shoulders, reaching up with his other meaty hand to gently rest it on the top of the goat's head. Haering appeared and stepped over to flank the animal. Ask nodded at the two men and knelt down, muttering reassurances to the goat as he drew his knife from its sheath on his belt.

The three of them moved in unison. Bergr and Haering grabbed the goat, grasping its head by the horns and using their limbs to brace its body to try and prevent it from moving overmuch. Ask cut across its throat and jugular vein in a single, easy stroke. Quickly dropping the stained knife, Ask scooped up a prepared bowl that had been sitting off to one side. Holding it under the wound, he collected the lifesblood as it gushed forth. The animal tried to bleat in distress, gurgling as it fought against the two large men that restrained it, but they held firm. The bowl filled quickly, but long seconds passed before the animal's struggles slowed and its head drooped, its life slipping away.

Ask rose to his feet and whispered a short prayer to the Lesir over the carcass. Turning, he strode back towards where Houngan Igul and Jarl Løgur stood, the brimming bowl cradled carefully in both hands. The jarl turned to face him, still smiling. Ask presented him with the bowl and the spirit lifted it to his lips, tilting his head back as he drained the contents in a single long swallow.

The Lesir exhaled loudly, smacking his lips appreciatively. 'Thank you, young hounsis.' He paused for a second. 'It will be houngan tonight, though, will it not? Houngan Ask.'

Ask nodded. 'If it pleases you, Jarl.'

'I take it you approve of his initiation then, Jarl?' Houngan Igul said.

Creasing his forehead, the jarl tapped his chin thoughtfully and let out a long 'hmmm' as he eyed Ask. After a few moments, he lifted the bowl he had just drained and placed it carefully upside-down on Ask's head. With great effort, Ask did not react. He knew from experience that much of what the old spirit did was just to try to provoke a reaction. Jarl Løgur cocked his head to one side, seeming to consider something, then nodded to himself and reached out to tilt the bowl so it sat at a slightly jaunty angle.

The three of them stood in silence for a few long seconds. Ask could feel a trickle of goat's blood slowly make its way down the side of his face. His eye twitched involuntarily. Houngan Igul was the first to crack, letting out a snort that quickly turned into a loud guffaw. He clapped Jarl Løgur on the shoulder and Ask started to chuckle as well. A number of the other villagers joined in and the jarl nodded again, his wide smile returning to his face.

Shaking his head, Houngan Igul took Ask by the arm and led him to the wooden bench that he would need to lie down on for the next part of the ceremony. As they walked, Ask reached up and gingerly removed the bowl and now-ruined scarf from his head.

Igul glanced over his shoulder, still smiling. 'That was surprisingly tame for the old jarl. You are very lucky.'

Ask grinned back but said nothing. He'd met Jarl Løgur a handful of times so far and the spirit seemed to have taken a liking to him; a good sign for his future as a houngan. Løgur was the head of the largest and most powerful family of Lesir, the spirits that the people of the Sundered Land paid homage to. Many of the Lesir were friendly and open, though none that Ask had met so far were quite as irreverent and eccentric as Jarl Løgur.

Behind them, a dozen villagers had crowded around the jarl seeking advice, assistance and insight into the fate the wyrd had laid out for them. Ask sat down on the bench and watched them for a few moments. Bergr gave the jarl a gift of a bottle of strong mead that Ask knew he'd been saving for a while. The spirit unstoppered it and drained the entire thing without taking a breath, then thanked the warrior for his gift. Isond brought over a small wicker basket filled with tiny, potent dried chili peppers. Jarl Løgur ate them a handful at a time as he spoke and laughed.

Ask smiled at the slightly bewildered expression on Isond's face as the spirit brazenly flirted with her. Fulnir, of course, had never been half as forward when he was courting her. It must have been disconcerting for her to hear the sorts of things the jarl was saying coming out of Fulnir's mouth.

Beside him, Houngan Igul took up a leather case and unfolded it to reveal a ceramic pot of ink and set of long, steel needles. Ask's stomach tightened when he glanced over and saw the tools. Houngan Igul had already told him that it was going to hurt, but actually seeing the needles brought his nervousness sharply back into focus. He averted his eyes, looking up at the sky as he gingerly lay back on the bench. The temporary relief from pain that the ceremony had given him was gone and Ask was acutely aware of each wound on his back. He tried to avoid putting too much of his weight on them, but that seemed to fail miserably. At least there was a layer of leather and fur between them and the rough wood of the bench.

Igul sat down cross-legged next to Ask's head and placed one hand gently on his shoulder.

'Relax. Are you ready?'

Ask nodded and closed his eyes. He took a deep breath as Igul scoured his face with a frigid cloth, cleaning it. Then his old master began the lengthy process of tattooing his face. The houngan pressed the side of his hand against Ask's cheek, resting the side of the needle against it as he repeatedly jabbed the point down into Ask's skin.

The needle stung. At first, it was a struggle to keep from flinching. Time dragged, but after a while he began to grow used to the stabbing sensation, even when Houngan Igul began working around his eye. Once it was completed, the intricate whorl of runic patterns across his right cheek and encircling his eye would mark him as a houngan. He would be Igul's equal instead of his apprentice. They took short breaks every ten minutes or so, so that Ask could stretch his facial muscles and blink his eyes.

'Draw a manhood here, next to his eye, as if it were about to poke him.'

Ask had his eyes closed and hadn't heard him approach, but it made sense for Jarl Løgur to inspect the tattoo design as it was being inscribed. Of course, the jarl was only joking. He was known for his crude sense of humour. Even knowing what the spirit was playing at, it was hard for Ask to see the comedy in the situation while at the receiving end of Houngan Igul's needle.

'Yes, yes! Just like that! The balls should be bigger, though, and do not forget the hair!'

Ask struggled to maintain his composure. The jarl was teasing to see if he could get a reaction, he told himself. He knew that that was the case. Houngan Igul had warned him beforehand that Jarl Løgur liked to do things like this.

'A wise choice, Jarl,' said Igul. 'Perhaps you would like to finish this part of the design yourself?'

Were he not already holding as still as he could, Ask would have frozen.

'It has been such a long time since I have tattooed someone, my hands are not as steady as they once were. Ah, very well, houngan! You have convinced me!'

The needle lifted from Ask's face as his eyes flew open in shock. Houngan Igul looked down at him with a smile, patting him reassuringly on the shoulder. 'The jarl will take over for a while, then. I will go to read the entrails of the sacrifice before it is cooked.'

Were they serious? Ask couldn't tell. If he said something, he might offend the jarl. If he didn't… Who knew what the old spirit would draw on him? The jarl dropped down onto the bench, Houngan Igul handed him his tools and he moved Ask's head into position where he could reach him. 'Ready?'

After a few moments of conflicting emotions wrestling for dominance, Ask decided to play along and closed his eyes, praying to the Lesir that he wasn't really about to end up with vulgar images drawn across his face. The needle descended and stabbed into his flesh once more. Ask was surprised by the Jarl's quick, precise movements. It was immediately obviously that the spirit knew his craft.

After a while Igul returned, swapping places with the jarl once again and sending the spirit sauntering back towards the other villagers. Ask could hear laughter and merriment, backed by the beating of drums. In his mind, he could see them dancing. The celebration was continuing without him, the Innsmen and jarl occupying themselves while they waited.

His tattoo was nearing completion when the appetising smell of cooking meat reached Ask's nostrils. He realised he was ravenously hungry. While Ask had his eyes closed, Igul must have signalled someone to skin and gut the goat they had used in the ceremony so it would be cooked and ready to be eaten when they were finished.

Finally, Igul put down his needle and Ask heard him crack his knuckles. 'Not bad at all,' the old houngan said, sounding pleased with himself.

'I'm starving,' Ask said.

He opened his eyes and stretched his facial muscles gingerly. They were sore from the sting of the needle and the effort of holding still for three hours. It hurt to so much as crack a smile.

More concerning was the work the Jarl had done. He was fairly certain that the spirit and Igul had simply been trying to rile him up and provoke a reaction, but he still had an anxious knot in his stomach that would not ease until he saw his reflection. Ask pulled himself up, being careful not to accidentally tear the stitches in his back.

'Good. There will be plenty of food and drink this night.'

Ask turned to look at his mentor seriously for a moment. 'Thank you, houngan. For everything.'

'Just Igul, now,' the older man admonished gently, smiling. 'No longer hounsis and mentor—we are brothers.'

'Thank you…Igul,' Ask said, and the old man's eyes twinkled.

Ask looked over at the revellers. Bergr had taken up his bone flute, joining Eydis and Isond as they drummed away. Haering had abandoned his own drum, joining the headsman and a small group of the other men as they laughed and boasted. By the warrior's gestures, it seemed as though he was telling of their hunting of the tokoloshe again. Someone had broken out a barrel of mead.

Several of the villagers had broken from the group and were busily cooking the goat, preparing stew and other foods. Nothing from the animal would be wasted— slaughtering an animal even at the tail end of winter was highly unusual, but it had been necessary for the ceremony.

Jarl Løgur caught his eye, waving them over. Igul folded up his leather case of needles and ink, tucking it under his arm as he stood. The two of them walked over to join the rest of the Innsmen. As they approached, the jarl stepped over to meet them and grasped Ask's left hand. Next to him, Igul took Ask's right and both of them lifted his arms in the air in a triumphant gesture. The gathered Innsmen bellowed their approval, letting out great whoops and cat-calls to celebrate. Ask heard a few voices call out 'Houngan Ask!' Though it hurt his face to do so, he grinned.

Igul let go of Ask's hand and retrieved a small, polished steel mirror from the leather case, holding it so that Ask could see his reflection. Ask turned his head this way and that, taking in the details. He breathed a sigh of relief, the tension in his stomach easing. The tattoo was an intricate, runic pattern that whorled around his eye and down across his cheek. There were some traces of ink that Igul had failed to wipe away still obscuring some small parts of it, and his flesh was an angry red, but it was enough to tell how it looked. Ask was pleased. In a couple of days it would look magnificent.

Each mambo and houngan's tattoo was a unique creation that spoke of what their mentor believed to be their strongest qualities. In his design, Igul had heavily emphasised Ask's loyalty and courage, with references to great strength and fortitude, both physical and spiritual. In this way, Ask's new markings were similar to Igul's own. There were also some marks that alluded to prowess at the seeking of and destruction of evil.

Those particular marks would have been inspired by hunt of the tokoloshe. It was customary for the tattoo to include a reference to the last deed that had finally convinced the mentor that his apprentice was ready to become a full priest—it was considered prophetic, a taste of what the future would bring for them.

Next to him, Jarl Løgur turned to regard the tattoo himself, smiling in approval. 'It is a good mark. Strong. The mark of a warrior. A protector.'

'Thank you, Jarl.' Ask took a deep breath then turned to face the crowd, raising his voice above the din. 'I make my oath now, to forever serve the people of this land and protect them from evil, faithfully and unceasingly.'

There was another roar of approval in response.

Igul handed his leather case and mirror off to someone to hold before reaching into his robe and drawing forth Ask's asson. The two of them had made it earlier, after the purification ritual that had taken up most of the day. The chants and rituals that went into the creation of a true asson were secrets imparted only to those being initiated as a mambo or houngan. The rattle was made of a hollowed out, fire-hardened gourd—ash-black and strung with wooden beads. Inside, Ask had placed specially-prepared stones carved with runic sigils and the knucklebones and teeth of the tokoloshe they had killed. Along with the tattoos, the asson was the symbol of a priest. It was the tool that he would use to lead ceremonies invoking the Lesir and as a focus to enhance and channel spiritual energy.

Ask bowed his head to Igul and took the asson reverentially, securing it in a leather thong hanging at his belt for that purpose.

'Lastly…' Jarl Løgur said quietly, placing a hand on his shoulder and turning him to look in his eyes.

Ask paused, unsure of what the jarl intended. The Lesir's face assumed a mask of concentration. Ask was suddenly aware of a massive well of spiritual power. His eyes widened. The jarl was expertly and seemingly effortlessly manipulating more energy than Ask had ever felt gathered in one place before. Not only that, he had channelled it so subtly and quickly that Ask hadn't even felt it build. It felt as though there was suddenly a great ocean wave poised to crash down on top of him, and the jarl was casually holding it back with only a little effort.

Reaching out, Jarl Løgur gently tapped Ask between the eyes. The world exploded. Ask couldn't see.

The pains in his back and face had vanished, conspicuous in their absence, and though his body felt strangely weightless he found he couldn't move. A flash of white light blinded him, but he couldn't close his eyes, couldn't even feel his eyelids. Then he could see again. A grey, foggy expanse spread out before him. Beneath his feet were dunes of ash, blown by an unfelt wind. He couldn't see more than a dozen yards ahead through the swirling greyness. Above him, a black, empty void stretched away into eternity.

He was alone at first, but then he wasn't. A man stood before him, staff raised defiantly to the heavens. There was a flash of golden light. A burning halo engulfed the man as a massive three-fingered hand, thin dark-grey digits with four knobbly knuckles—each a dozen yards apart—descended upon the both of them.

The golden light spiked to meet the hand and there was a sound, so deep and loud that Ask could barely hear it. It was like the blare of a massive horn blown directly into his ear, but the noise was distorted and lowered until it was more pressure than sound, and set his teeth to vibrating in his skull. It was painful, but it was as though the pain was happening to someone else. Someone else's eardrums were bursting. Someone else felt like the sound was shaking their body apart.

Above them, a massive, dark shape blotted out the sky. The owner of the hand. Ask realised what the sound was. It was a roar. A bellow of surprise and sudden anger. The gigantic hand plunged towards him. Everything went black.

Ask jerked back. He was standing in Innset again as Jarl Løgur lowered his hand. He blinked a couple of times and almost fell backwards, but Igul steadied him with a reassuring hand gripping his bicep.

'Easy,' Igul said.

'What was *that*?'

'A gift.' Jarl Løgur grinned widely, but it seemed more like he was baring his teeth than smiling.

'I don't understand.' Ask shook his head, trying to sort out what had just happened. 'What did I just see?'

The jarl dismissed his question with a wave of his hand. 'Now is not the time. Now, we celebrate!' He stepped away from Ask, taking a horn of mead from the hand of a nearby Innsman and heading towards the spitted goat.

Igul patted Ask on the arm. 'It is nothing to be concerned about. Not yet, in any case. We can talk later. Relax and enjoy yourself for now.'

Ask shot him an anxious look, but nodded. He gratefully took a drinking horn when it was offered to him and took a swig to calm his jangling nerves. The vision had shaken him, but he tried to push it to the back of his mind and focus on the night ahead of him.

- - -

Exhausted by the celebrations, Ask took the opportunity to rest by the dying embers of the bonfire as the evening began to wind down. Stuffed full of good food and mead, he let himself relax and simply watch the others talking and laughing as he nursed his horn of drink in one hand. It felt as though every single person in the village had wanted to congratulate him personally. His belt and cloak were decorated with small tokens and gifts meant to bring him luck.

Ask took another slow sip of mead and watched Erlend gesticulate wildly with outstretched hands as he spoke, his conversation with several other Innsmen growing more heated. The headsman's great, booming laugh split the evening like a roll of thunder. A chorus of guffaws and exclamations echoed in its wake. In the dancing light of the torches that ringed the area, Ask could just make out Fulnir and Isond standing at the far side of the village centre, half-shadowed under the eaves of her home.

Haering was over talking to a few of the village women. He glanced over, having noticed Ask's gaze, and raised his horn of mead slightly in a silent toast. Ask smiled and mimicked the gesture. His adoptive father said a few quick words to the women, bobbing his head respectfully, then walked over.

'Houngan Ask,' he rumbled, a touch of pride in his tone.

'Haering,' Ask said, bobbing his head awkwardly in acknowledgement. He felt off-balance. Haering had practically raised him, and it felt odd that his surrogate father was now expected to show him the respect due to a houngan. There was an awkward pause, which Ask broke after a few seconds of silence. 'I did not have a chance to thank you the other day. You saved my life.'

The bearlike man shook his head. 'You saved yourself, with the Lesir's guidance. All I can hope is that Grein had a smile on his face when Jarl Dauðvís came to collect him, knowing that his axe slew the monster that killed him.'

'I just wish we had realised what was happening earlier. His death could have been avoided, and Asa...'

26

Haering shook his head, then glanced over to where Igul stood, near the headsman. After confirming they were unobserved, he hunkered down and lowered his voice conspiratorially. 'You did good,' he said, warm mead on his breath. 'Houngan Igul was right; we would not have caught that thing if you had not chased it down the way you did. I may have been holding the axe, but it was you that killed that monster, no mistake. We have been blessed by the Lesir to have a pair of houngans as strong as you two.'

Ask's cheeks burned. He looked down, unable to help the smile that crept across his face. 'I will try to do my best.'

'You will be wanting to do some travelling soon, I imagine.' Haering nudged him with a shoulder.

'Soon.' Ask looked up and nodded. 'I am in no great rush. Perhaps in a few weeks' time.'

'Fair.' Haering struggled back to his feet. Pausing for a moment, he looked back down at Ask and raised his drinking horn again. 'Your father would have been a proud man, had he lived to see his son grown.' He grinned, bobbed his head again, then turned on his heel and sauntering back towards the others.

Ask finished his drink, watching the antics of the rest of the Innsmen. The last few days had been an intense blur; he was glad to finally get some time to relax. After a while, Igul came over to where he sat. Gingerly, the older man lowered himself to the ground to sit beside Ask, dropping his heavy ironwood staff at his feet. 'How fare your injuries?'

'Sore, but I will live,' Ask said.

'You will do better than that, if I am any judge.'

Ask nodded, more to reassure himself than his mentor. 'I hope I do not disappoint you.'

They sat in silence, enjoying the quiet companionship. Ask smiled to himself when Fulnir and Isond disappeared off into the darkness together. Beside him, Igul snorted in amusement. 'To be young again. Why are you not with a woman tonight? I thought that the Faraldsdottir girl was sweet on you.'

Ask glanced over to where Lif Faraldsdottir stood, conversing with her younger sister Verun and Eydis. She saw him look at her and shot him back a venomous glare before pointedly turning back to her companions and ignoring him. 'Lif...I think she liked the idea of marrying a houngan more than she actually liked me.'

Igul chuckled quietly. 'Ah well. At least my remaining apprentice is taking full advantage of the virility of youth.'

'When did the jarl leave?'

'A while ago, I think. It is hard to tell sometimes. You were fortunate that Fulnir was the one Løgur chose to mount. If it had been me, he may have insisted on doing the entire tattooing himself. Who knows if he would have restrained himself quite as much then? And if he had mounted you, you may well have ended up with marks like Hafgrim.'

'Like Hafgrim?' Ask's forehead creased, his thoughts shifting to the conspicuously absent houngan.

'Look closely at his tattoos when next you see him,' Igul said. He leant back and looked up at the stars, a smile on his face. 'Løgur mounted him during his initiation and refused to sit still the entire time. I thought old Hakon was going to have a fit.'

'Hafgrim did not come today. The boy that Erlend sent has not returned, either,' Ask said. 'It has only been a day and a half, but still...'

'You have an ill feeling,' said Igul. The older man's expression turned serious. He was silent for handful of seconds and the pause sent a shiver of anxiety through Ask. 'Tokoloshe are scavengers. Wicked pranksters. They revel in creating confusion and mischief, but they are vulnerable and weak on their own.

'Under ordinary circumstances one would not openly harass a community protected by a mambo or houngan unless there was something more dangerous nearby that had attracted it, or if it were in thrall to a bokor,' he said, stroking his beard absently with one hand. 'We cornered the creature in the woods to the west of here. Engerdal also lies in that direction.'

Ask frowned. 'You think that Hafgrim is dealing with his own problems.'

'I think that Erlend sent a runner to Engerdal two days ago and we have not heard back. I think that tokoloshe always means that more trouble is brewing. And I believe I read portents of great evil and darkness in the entrails of the goat we sacrificed this evening.'

It was Ask's turn to be silent for a moment as he let the implications sink in. Patterns in the wyrd divined using the entrails of a slaughtered animal were often vague, but always reliable. 'Did you speak to the Jarl about the reading?' he asked.

Igul nodded, 'I did. He was not clear, as is the way of the Lesir, but what he did say worried me. Fulnir and I will be leaving for Engerdal in the morning.'

'Fulnir and you? Not me?'

'If you wish to accompany us you are welcome to, of course,' Igul said. The corners of his mouth had turned up slightly and there was a light note in his voice. 'You are a houngan. It is for you to decide what your wisest course of action is.'

'I...'

Ask had no idea how to respond to that. His mentor remained quiet, his eyes twinkling in amusement. At first, Ask thought Igul was teasing him, but after a few seconds he realised that all the older man was doing was encouraging him to take up his new responsibilities as a houngan and think for himself. He had to start thinking like a houngan. 'If there is something out there stopping travel between the villages, something strong enough to stop Houngan Hafgrim from even contacting us, confronting it will be dangerous.'

'True.'

Ask hesitated. The tokoloshe had wrought such havoc before they had hunted it down. It had only been a minor spirit, but it had killed two people. And Asa would likely never recover from the torments it had inflicted upon her. 'If I go with you, Innset will be vulnerable. Another tokoloshe, or something worse, may rear its head.'

'Also true.'

He sighed. Igul wasn't going to be any help, it seemed. After a few moments of silence, his mind stewing over his first real decision as a houngan, Ask made up his mind. 'It is clear where my responsibilities lie, then,' he said, his voice sounding much more confident than he felt. 'I will remain here to watch over Innset.'

Igul smiled and nodded. 'Very well, if I am able to determine that the path between the villages is safe, I will send a runner back once Fulnir and I have arrived in Engerdal.'

Stifling a yawn, Ask drained the last dregs of mead from his horn and dropped the emptied vessel casually to the furs beside him. He looked over at his mentor, his expression pensive. 'That vision I had earlier, when the jarl touched me. It was some sort of divination,' he said. 'What exactly did he do?'

'The jarl reached as far forward into the wyrd as he could and gave you a true telling of your own future.'

Ask rocked back as though he had been slapped. 'A true telling...'

'It was a part of your initiation. Only mambos and houngans are allowed to know of this,' Igul said. His voice had dropped low enough to be inaudible to any of the others nearby. 'I do not know what you saw, but the jarl is strong enough to reach for the end of your life. Most see exactly how they will die.'

Ask shivered, his hands and back suddenly clammy with a cold sweat. It almost didn't seem possible. 'The Lesir can do that?'

'It is not something done lightly. Divining the wyrd is difficult even under ideal conditions, as you well know. Even then, getting more than vague impressions of the near future requires much power and skill.' Igul shifted slightly so that he could turn and watch the coals of the bonfire before continuing. 'A true telling is something only the wisest and strongest can attempt. I have never managed it myself, but I have spoken to others stronger than I who have.'

'I think I saw one of the Faceless.'

Igul paused, his eyes widening slightly. When he spoke again, his words were quiet and measured. 'Are you sure?'

Ask pulled his knees up to his chest, not meeting his mentor's gaze. The aching of his injured back suddenly seemed more intense, his mind desperately trying to use it to distract him from what he was about to say. 'I've never heard of anything else that size. I'm not sure where I was…it was difficult to see clearly. It cannot have been, can it? The Lesir would not allow it.' He glanced over at Igul. 'The true telling, how does it work? Did the jarl see what I saw?'

'I am unsure. If he does, he makes no indication of it,' Igul said.

'Should I talk to him about it? Or one of the other Lesir?'

The old man combed the fingers of one hand through the white-grey hair of his beard, the corners of his mouth turning up slightly. 'The true telling was yours,' he said Ask. 'You decide what to do with what you were shown. What you saw was a piece of the wyrd itself. You cannot change it, but you can prepare for it.'

Ask watched as more revellers staggered off to collapse in their homes. Light streaks of pink and orange were starting to glow at the horizon. Today was his first day as a houngan, an initiated priest of the Lesir. With Igul and Fulnir leaving for Engerdal, the men and women of Innset would be depending solely on him for spiritual counsel and protection. People would be looking to him for guidance and advice, but he felt as though he barely knew anything at all. It felt far from real. Even after so many years living and learning as Igul's hounsis, he wasn't sure he was ready to bear the weight of the responsibility that was being thrust on his shoulders.

He swallowed hard, thinking again about the true telling that the jarl had given him. Had the giant he had seen truly been one of the Faceless? The *jayen*? He had no idea. Brow furrowed, he looked back over at Igul. 'What was your true telling?'

Igul inclined his head. 'In my experience, most mambos and houngans reach the end of their life in the same way. Through violence. Rare is the one that lives to see himself lying in bed, dying of old age.'

'Is that what you saw?'

'No,' he said.

The old man dug the end of his staff into the ground to help him stand up, looking around at the steadily lightening village and avoiding Ask's inquiring gaze. 'I'm going to get a few hours of rest before we leave this morning. Good night, houngan.'

- - -

Ask woke with a start, some odd feeling shaking him from sleep. Light filtered in through gaps in the wooden slats that covered the only window of the cramped room, shafts of brightness that told him the day was already well started. Blinking a few times to clear the blur from his eyes, he pulled himself into a sitting position, pushing away the pile of furs. It felt unusual, to him, to be rising this late in the day. Houngan Igul had been harsh regarding the hour he expected his hounsis to be awake and ready to confront the day. Ask's body drooped slightly, tempting him to bask in his newfound freedom and indulge in a bit of post-initiation laziness. He let out a sigh, resisting the lure of sleep, and forced himself to stand. It had been four days since his initiation.

What little illumination seeped through the gaps in the window slats lent Ask just enough light to see by in the otherwise-dark room. He carefully stepped over toward the door, stumbling and cursing when something small and sharp dug into the sole of one foot. Limping slightly, he shoved the door open with the heel of his hand, letting a sudden burst of light stream into the house. He hunkered down next to the small bundle of clothes that had been stuffed in a corner near the fire pit.

Houngan Igul's house was unremarkable amongst the others in the small village; wooden, dug-in dwellings with heavily-layered straw thatch for roofing, clustered tightly together for protection. Each was a single room with no interior walls, with the exception of the headsman's house, and served as a home for an entire family.

However, while Igul's was much the same size as the others, inside there was barely enough room to move around. The centre of the room was occupied by a fire pit dug down into the earth a handspan and lined with flat shards of slate. The walls were hung with coloured cloths stitched with the veves of individual Lesir, the jarls' runic symbols displayed proudly above their respective altars. Small spaces between the altars were piled with furs where Igul, Fulnir and Ask slept. Every other part of the room was cluttered with the paraphernalia of their craft. Row upon row of dried plants hung from the ceiling, medicinal and otherwise; they gave off a riotous mix of aromas that often made the eyes of visitors water.

As a houngan, Ask would be entitled to call on the Innsmen's assistance to help build him a house of his own if he chose to stay on in Innset. Part of him was thrilled to have finally earned a position of respect among the villagers and was eager to set about establishing himself. On the other hand, it was not uncommon for newly-initiated houngans and mambos to spend some time travelling before settling in a particular location.

Igul had never expounded on his own time spent exploring the Sundered Land. Even so, Ask knew that it had only been two dozen years ago that his mentor had settled in Innset.

Ask himself had never strayed further from Innset than the neighbouring villages of Engerdal and Billingstad. His apprenticeship to Igul took up most of his time, and he had little family to speak of. During the winter, the young warriors among the Innsmen normally met up with the others from the nearby villages and set out across the channel that separated the peninsula from the Jewelled Islands. Normally they would set out from Billingstad, on the coast. Piled into the longboats that served as fishing vessels during the warmer months, they would raid the coastal settlements of the Jewelled Islands, taking what plunder they could and returning once the season began to turn.

This winter, however, Innset had been plagued with a rash of accidents and deaths. A small handful of men who would normally have headed off to join the winter raiding had remained behind to help Houngan Igul safeguard the village against whatever malefic force was behind it.

Ask dressed himself in the light from the doorway, pulling on a pair of dark woollen trousers and a simple off-white tunic. A thin jacket of mottled calfskin leather went over the top along with a rust-red woollen cloak, which he secured in place with an iron brooch. As he slid on his boots, he heard a woman's voice call his name. He turned his head as he tied the straps of the boots and saw Isond heading in his direction. Straightening up, he smiled and gave a small wave.

'Ask!' Isond said, slowing to a halt just in front of him. 'I wanted to talk to you.'

'What is the matter?'

Isond seemed to remember herself, dipping her head. 'Sorry. Houngan. I wanted to ask about Houngan Igul. Has there been any word from Engerdal?'

It had been four days since Houngan Igul and Fulnir had set out for the nearby village, and Ask was beginning to fear the worst. No runner had yet returned to Innset with news. 'Not yet,' he said. 'Houngan Igul will send word when he believes it safe to do so.'

'Something might have happened to them.' Isond frowned at him. 'It's been days. Are you not going to go after them?'

'I know you worry about Fulnir. He will be fine. They have probably encountered some sort of problem, but Igul knows what he is doing.' He made to walk past her, but she stepped in front of him.

'We could get together a hunting band, like Houngan Igul did for that monster,' she persisted. 'Haering and Bergr and my mother. We could all go and make sure.'

If whatever had attracted the tokoloshe to the region had overwhelmed Igul, Ask was not confident that he would fare any better. On the other hand, if whatever darkness had fallen over the region had claimed both Hafgrim and Igul, it was a serious threat and action needed to be taken. He had already started considering either going after Igul or sending a message to the mambos that watched over nearby Billingstad, but had come to no decision as yet. So far, he had been hiding his own worry for the sake of the other Innsmen, but as the days passed it had been gnawing at him constantly.

Ask sighed. Isond was right. 'Very well. I will consult with the Lesir this morning and ask for their guidance. See if you can round up some of the others and come and see me at midday and I will share the spirit's wisdom.'

Ask didn't foresee her having any difficulty in getting the Innsmen interested. Now that the tokoloshe had been dealt with, the few who had missed the raiding expeditions had little to occupy their time.

'Thank you, houngan.' Isond dipped her head again before turning away.

Ask bent to scoop up a battered wooden bucket that lay discarded near the door, discreetly watching as she left. He had grown up with Isond; it felt awkward for her to address him so formally. Isond lapsed, here and there, forgetting that he was a houngan and talking to him as she normally would have. To be honest, he felt a lot more comfortable with that than with her bowing her head all the time.

Starting toward the river, Ask glanced up at the sky, gauging how long he had been asleep by the position of the sun. He could ask Erlend to send runners to Billingstad or even Heggedal, he mused as he walked. If the threat was dire, he would need help from someone more experienced. Then again, he did not want a false alarm to set the tone for his time as a houngan.

Signy was on her way back from the river with a pair of large buckets brimming with water slung over her shoulders. Ask was impressed at how effortless the older woman made it look. Signy was on the verge of becoming a great grandmother, but the muscles under her wrinkled skin were strong as steel. She grinned at Ask as he went to pass her. "Houngan! Fine morning to you.'

'To you as well,' Ask said. 'Tell me, how is Asa?'

'She will live.' Signy stopped and shook her head. 'The poor girl has been through a lot. That *monskellr* was vicious. I would have liked to cut the thing down myself.'

The older woman had been a formidable warrior in her day. Igul had asked her to join the hunt they'd gone on, but she had told him that taking care of Asa was more important than traipsing off into the forest chasing monsters. Very few Innsmen would talk back to Igul that way. Ask liked her.

'We may need to go on another hunt. Would you join us?'

She shot him a distinctly unimpressed look. 'I will come if you need me, but Asa still needs looking after.'

Ask smiled. 'Then that is more important. Take care of her.'

'I will.' Signy straightened her back and continued onward.

Small clumps of ice at the edges of the riverbank where the current was weakest made the footing treacherous but navigable. After filling his bucket with the frigid water, Ask returned to Igul's house, taking care not to slop any on himself.

Ask took a clean cloth and used some of the water to wash his face and neck. He left the door open while he rummaged amongst his personal items and withdrew a bundle wrapped in cloth, dyed the same rust-red as his cloak. There was just enough clear space for him to unroll it and he took care not to let any of the items inside drop out as he spread the cloth on the floor. A runic veve, the symbol of Hyrr Lorajaðr, was stitched in black thread across the cloth. With so little space in Igul's home, there had never been enough room for his hounsis to set up their own altars to the

Lesir. Instead, they had made do with temporary ones, taking them out when needed and packing them away after performing their offerings.

Ask lit a small tallow candle and placed it on the makeshift altar. He arranged the offerings he had previously made to Hyrr Lorajaðr around it; a sharp iron dagger, a pouch of dried chili peppers, a small goat's horn carved to resemble a wolf, and a wide iron ring cut with runes. These were only the most recent gifts he had presented the Lesir with. It was traditional to dispose of past offerings once a reasonable length of time had passed, sooner if they were foodstuffs, and Ask had gotten into a rhythm of clearing out his own every six months. Lorajaðr liked his offerings to be buried in the forest at the base of a tree.

Ask leant over the hut's central fire pit, poking at the coals inside. They were still smouldering. It would have been troublesome to have to start a fire from scratch. During the winter months, everyone tried not to let their fires burn out completely. The smouldering material glowed weakly with threads of orange and red. Ask nurtured the flame, using more tinder and then a small amount of kindling to coax it to life. The wood was dry and wisps of smoke fled the hut through the vent in the roof.

Ask sat down cross-legged, his back to the door, and stared over the altar into the fire. He focused on his breathing, emptying his mind of distractions and letting himself relax. The aches in his back began to melt away as he meditated on the dancing flames. Absently, he leant forward and took up a handful of sticks, feeding them to the fire and letting his hand linger over the heat. Tongues of flame seemed to reach up to tickle his open palm. He lowered his hand. It was hot, but not unpleasantly so. Ask's patron,

Lorajaðr, was of the Hyrr family of Lesir. The Hyrr embodied aspects of fire and so the flame would not hurt Ask if he did not wish it to.

Selecting a small flask of honey mead from a cluttered shelf, just within arm's reach, Ask held it in front of him with two hands, still staring into the flames.

'*Hyrr Jarl Virding, tanpri ouvri nan pòtay lavil la. Mwen prezante w ak yon ofrann epi mande pou benediksyon ou.*'

Ask took a breath and repeated himself in the Old Tongue, 'Jarl Virding, please open the gate. I give you this gift and ask for your blessing.'

This, at least, was one part of being a houngan he was completely at ease with. He had performed this ritual and others like it a thousand times, and the small eddies of energy that he could feel pulling at him were comforting in their familiarity.

An overwhelming pressure pushed down on him, as though an invisible but solid presence had suddenly flooded the room. It was stifling, but not unpleasant. He touched the offering to his forehead, his lips, then his crotch before placing it between the altar to Lorajaðr and the fire pit.

'It has been ten days since I last brought you an offering, great jarl, and I will bring another ten days hence. In return, please open the gate for me.'

The pressure vanished, replaced by a disorienting feeling of space and openness. Ask's stomach leaped into his chest as he became aware of a gulf stretching out around him, as though he stood upon the precipice of a great cliff. The jarl's spirit poked at him with a sensation of greeting and mirth. He steadied Ask's spirit, anchoring him to something hard and unyielding that enveloped them both. Despite its seeming solidity, Ask's mind perceived the structure as a barely-there shimmer, almost like a heat haze, flecked with multi-coloured hues—*Lakansyèl*, the Rainbow Bridge.

The spirit was still there, but it had faded into the background, its attention turned elsewhere.

'Thank you, great jarl,' Ask said, and there was a flickering feeling of acknowledgement in return. Ask concentrated on his breathing for a few moments before speaking again. '*Hyrr Lorajaðr Virdingsson, mwen chache fòs kouraj ou.* I seek your strength, son of Jarl Virding. Hear me and answer.'

The presence of Jarl Virding was an all-pervading pressure, a blanket of power pressing down upon those who petitioned him. When his son Lorajaðr came, however, it was as though Ask was standing too near a bolt of lightning as it struck the earth. The hair on the back of his neck and on his arms stood on end, a phantom smell of ozone scouring his nostrils. Hyrr Lorajaðr was a warrior spirit, protector of the Sundered Land and master of thunder and lightning. His strength and power was obvious in every interaction Ask had ever had with him.

Ask's hand trembled slightly as he grabbed the offering he had prepared earlier, a blackened knot of hard wood from a lightning split tree, carved with secret words of the Old Tongue. His fingers felt clumsy and he fumbled it slightly before mimicking the gesture he had made earlier, touching it to his forehead, his lips and his crotch.

'I bring you this gift, Lorajaðr, and in return I ask for guidance,' Ask said.

He placed the offering on the altar, careful not to jostle any of the others. 'Hougan Igul left for Engerdal four days ago to seek out Houngan Hafgrim, yet we have heard nothing from either of them. Ill omens preceded the journey, portents of evil and darkness. Igul may require aid, but if I follow after him, Innset would be without spiritual protection should something happen in our absence. I could send a messenger to Billingstad to ask Mam Botvi and Mam Sida for aid or advice, but I...' Ask trailed off, hesitating.

It was pointless to be less than completely honest with any of the Lesir, but that didn't make it any easier to say certain things aloud. Lorajaðr was more than just a distant spirit—he was a friend. Ask had drunk with him, broken bread with him. He was a friend. It was hard to admit weakness in front of him. 'I do not know what to do,' Ask confessed after a moment of indecision. 'This is the first real decision I am making as a houngan. I feel as though I should be able to take care of it myself. If I lack confidence in myself the very first time I encounter a problem and go running to others for help, will I always, every time I need to make a decision?

'I am supposed to be a warrior, a protector. What if Igul requires aid, but I delay following him and doom him with my inaction? But then, what if something has already happened to Igul and Hafgrim, and by following after them I am only dooming myself and Innset? I am afraid of making the wrong choice.'

Hyrr Lorajaðr didn't respond right away and Ask felt a knot of anxiety form in his gut. The fire before him flared up, the flames stretching almost all the way to the roof of the hut. A surge of emotion from Lorajaðr hit Ask like a physical blow, hard enough to make him rock back.

While not physically present, the Lesir communicated through flashes of emotion and fragments of thoughts. Ask felt something that seemed like courage in the face of a great danger. Ferocity, bravery, battle-lust, determination. In front of him, figures danced within the fire. A call to arms. Proud warriors descending upon their enemies head-on, even though outnumbered and outmanoeuvred. Reinforcements summoned from all corners, catching the enemy between their forces. Battle. An uncertain outcome.

Ask took several deep breaths as the stream of emotion and visions faded. Afterimages flickered at the edge of seeing as he blinked and tried to wrest back control of his thundering heart. Lorajaðr projected reassurance and strength, extending a feeling of support, like that from the steadying hand of a comrade on Ask's shoulder.

He nodded slowly. 'I think I understand. Thank you. If the wyrd does lead me to battle, I will need your strength. Guide my weapon, fortify my body against harm. In return, I will anoint my fallen enemies with fire in your honour.' Ask paused to wait for a response.

The spirit quieted, not acknowledging the offer.

Ask hesitated a moment, taking a moment to decide on what he could add to the bargain that would please the Lesir. 'And, once I have returned to Innset, I will create a permanent altar dedicated to you to replace this one, as befitting your status as my patron.'

A sense of approval radiated from Lorajaðr, followed by another image flaring in the flames—a bolt of energy striking a tree.

'With a base made of lightning-split wood, as you request. If I do this, will you grant me your strength in the matter at hand?'

The Lesir withdrew, leaving only a lingering sense of strength and approval. Ask sat for a few moments as the presence retreated into the background of the spiritual infinity around him. It seemed Lorajaðr had accepted his bargain. Once his heart resumed a steady resting beat and his breathing was slow and normal, he lifted his hands. 'Hyrr Jarl Virding, thank you. I have asked all that needs to be asked. Please, close the gate.'

There was a feeling of claustrophobia and Ask's awareness immediately began to contract. The vast expanse shrunk around him until he could no longer feel the direct presence of the spirits or the reassuring anchor of *Lakansyèl*. In front of him, the fire flickered back down to smouldering embers, its fuel consumed. Ask rolled up the altar and its contents, standing and stowing it away once it had been tied shut.

The offering to Jarl Virding went into a pouch, which he then tied to his belt as he looped it around his waist. Ask would dispose of it in the woods on their way to Engerdal. He secured several other leather pouches to the belt, filling them with an assortment of materials for his craft, along with the leather thong that held his asson in easy reach. Ask took one last moment to look around, checking that there was nothing else he would need. Satisfied that he had everything, he stepped back out into the cool air and closed the door to Igul's hut behind him.

He was nervous. Lorajaðr had seemed confident, but he was always confident. Arrogant, even. But that was to be expected from a swaggering warrior spirit. Ask had always felt a little like he had been chosen by the wrong spirit, but there was no denying that he felt a kinship with Lorajaðr that went beyond their differences. He took a deep breath as he walked, trying to draw upon the spirit's confident to mask his own growing doubts.

- - -

44

The wheels of the wagon creaked quietly as the shaggy-maned horses pulled it, trudging through the foot of fresh snow that had fallen during the night. Ask rode at the head of the wagon. Next to him sat Eydis, reigns in her sundarkened hands and a sturdy axe at her side. Haering and Isond sat in the back, next to the supplies of food, water and various other things they had brought with them. Bergr walked briskly to keep pace beside them.

'Hold a moment,' Ask said, looking off to one side. Eydis pulled the horses to a stop immediately. Stepping down from his seat, the young houngan dropped to the snow and walked purposefully into the trees at the side of the path. Bergr made to follow, but stopped at a gesture and a shake of the head from Ask. He gave a slightly embarrassed smile before disappearing into the trees.

A dozen yards into the wood, Ask dropped to one knee at the foot of a tree chosen at random. Using both hands, he cleared away the snow from a patch of earth, cold snowmelt dampening his gloves. He retrieved a small trowel from his belt and dug into the frozen ground. After several seconds work, he returned the trowel to its place and exchanged it for the small flask of honeyed mead he had given as a gift to Hyrr Jarl Virding earlier that morning. He touched it to his forehead, his lips and his crotch, whispering the name of the Jarl, then dropped it into the hole and covered it over with dirt and snow.

Ask returned to the others, climbing back onto the wagon. Once they'd resumed their previous pace, Isond leaned over to speak with him. 'Is everything okay?' she asked.

He nodded. 'My apologies. It was nothing, I was just burying an offering.' Out of the corner of his eye, he could see Isond's hand tapping the haft of the axe next to her. 'We are still a ways off Engerdal. I do not expect any trouble until we are closer.'

Isond shifted her weight nervously. 'What are we expecting?'

'I do not know yet.'

'Could have fooled me,' she muttered. Her mother glanced back and gave her a pointed look. 'Er, forgive me, houngan. It is just, back with the others…'

Ask had to stop himself from shaking his head. He still wasn't quite used to everyone being so polite with him. 'It is fine. We should be prepared. Hyrr Lorajaðr indicated that there may be a malignant presence in Engerdal of some kind, but until we meet up with Houngan Igul we should not make assumptions.'

'As you say, houngan.' She sighed heavily. Leaning back in the wagon, she flicked her long braid forward over her shoulder.

'Did you check in on Asa before we left? How is she?' Ask said, changing the subject.

'Still shaken, but fine. She thought she was going mad, the way that evil spirit was tormenting her.'

'It was a vile creature,' Bergr added, his voice tight. 'Grein was a good man. I am only glad it did not get a chance to hurt or kill anyone else before we killed the thing.'

Ask nodded. 'If my suspicions are correct, its presence was not a coincidence. Something drew it here.'

'Another spirit? A stronger one?'

'Maybe,' he said. 'As I said, we should not make assumptions.'

Before they'd left Innset, Ask had spoken with Erlend and instructed him to send messengers to Mam Botvi and Mam Sida in Billingstad as well as the priests in Heggedal. He'd written missives on cured goat hide using a stick of charcoal, requesting aid be sent as a matter of urgency.

He'd tried to project confidence and reassurance when speaking to Erlend, but he wasn't sure he'd entirely succeeded. The visions from Lorajaðr had been strongly suggestive that there was a great evil in Engerdal and that Ask would require assistance in combating it. However, the form that the evil would take was less clear. Ask's patron always couched his responses in metaphors of fighting and bloodshed, so Ask had been quite liberal in his preparations, attempting to cover all possibilities.

They had left before midday the previous day and, under ordinary circumstances, they would have reached Engerdal this morning. As things stood, Ask had decided on a less direct route, circling around and approaching the village from a different direction than Igul would have. It cost them half a day, but if anything was watching for more travellers coming from the direction of Innset, it might give them a chance to get much closer before being detected.

- - -

The shadows were long, the sun creeping toward the horizon, when they approached an outlying farmstead. Ask motioned for the wagon to stop and they took a moment to take stock of the place from a distance before revealing themselves.

'This is Domar and Luta's place, yes?' asked Haering as they peered through the trees. The house was a wooden dug-in, much like the dwellings in Innset, but lower and longer. From here it wasn't clear whether it was one long hall or had two separate rooms.

'I think so,' said Isond. 'They usually come into the village square to trade. I have not come out to their farm before now, though.'

'Can you remember if they have children?' Ask narrowed his eyes at the farmstead. There were no signs of movement. No smoke came from the vent on the roof of the house, which was unusual at this hour. He concentrated, casting out his senses in an attempt to detect any evil presences, but found nothing.

'Two boys, I think. Hersir and Birgir? And a girl. I do not remember her name.'

Ask turned and looked back at her. 'I do not see anyone.' He cast his gaze over their small group, meeting everyone's eyes. 'It is late in the day, perhaps the children are in the barn taking care of the animals, but I do not see smoke from a cook fire and it seems too still and quiet.'

'Trouble?' Bergr asked quickly, worrying at the pendant at his neck with thumb and forefinger.

'Perhaps.' Ask was quiet for a moment before glancing at Haering. He wasn't a warrior, he had no idea how to approach situations like this. 'What should we do?' he asked his adopted father.

Haering was watching the farmstead closely. 'Bergr and I will go. The rest remain here. We will signal if it is safe to approach.'

'I will come, too,' said Ask, a touch of uncertainty in his tone.

'As will I.' Isond took a step forward to stand beside him.

'No,' said Haering. 'Stay here with your mother.'

Isond looked at Ask expectantly, but he shook his head. She answered with a small sound of frustration in the back of her throat, but stepped back toward the wagon. Her mother put a hand on her shoulder and whispered something to her as the three others started toward the farm. Bergr and Ask spread out to either side, letting Haering take the lead and staying fifteen feet to his left and right a few paces behind him.

Together, they made their way slowly toward the house, vigilant for any sign that things were amiss. As Haering moved toward the door, Ask glanced toward the barn. The doors were closed and he couldn't see inside from here. Still, he noted that last night's snow was still piled up outside the doors of both the barn and the house itself, as though they hadn't been opened all day.

It was eerily quiet. Even this close, there was little sound but his own footsteps and those of the men with him. The place seemed abandoned. Normally, the livestock would be making at least some noise.

No overt trouble having revealed itself, the three of them congregated around the door. Haering looked at Ask expectantly. After a moment's hesitation, the young houngan pounded on the door with a fist. There was no response. Bracing himself, Ask took hold of the handle in both hands and dragged it open, ploughing a furrow in the snow. As he stepped into the entryway, a musty smell of rot and human excrement met his nostrils. The weak evening light streamed in from behind him, giving just enough light to see the interior of the dwelling.

The house was one long hall, with a fire pit near to the middle and bedding clustered around it. Four lumpy shapes lay amongst the bedding; people either resting or dead. The nearest shifted slightly as the light touched it and a rough-spun woollen blanket fell from a shoulder to reveal a man's face, his features pallid and sunken. He let out a low moan.

'Get the others, stay outside,' Ask said, flicking his hand toward Bergr.

Without waiting for a reply, Ask covered his mouth with his palm, pinching his nostrils shut between his thumb and his forefinger, and marched into the house. He knelt down beside the man he assumed must be Domar and pulled back the blanket and furs, moving so that he did not block the light from the door. Even with his hand covering his mouth, he could taste the fresh wave of stench that rolled over him. Domar had soiled himself and, judging by his woollen trousers, crusted and stiff with dried urine and excrement, likely some time ago. The shirtless man moved his arm in what might have been a vague attempt at covering himself again and, when Ask took hold of his wrist to stop him, his skin was ice-cold and clammy with sweat.

Letting go of his arm, Ask reached up and slid his fingers behind Domar's head, angling the man's face so he could look at him. Using his thumb, he pulled on the skin below the man's eye, forcing it halfway open. The orb itself was glassy and unseeing, Domar either not trying or not able to focus on or look at him.

Ask fought the urge to take a deep breath to steady himself, forcing his intake of air to remain soft and shallow. Domar was ill, deathly so. He spared a glance over at the other bundles at the far side of the fire pit. Domar's family. Alive? Dead? Ask couldn't tell from here. Was it a plague? If so, Ask had already exposed himself to the risk of infection.

Carefully letting Domar's head drop, he took hold of the man's lower lip and pulled it down to examine his gums. They were pale, almost as white as the rest of his flesh, with a touch of grey where they met Domar's yellowed teeth.

Ask moved his hand to the man's chest, fingers spread. He focused on his awareness of his hand, pressing against the clammy, waxy skin and the smattering of dark hair that tickled his palm. Closing his eyes to block out visual distractions, he concentrated on the faint rising and falling of Domar's shallow breathing. After a handful of seconds crawled by he could feel the feeble, sluggish beat of the man's heart, though only barely.

Pushing past that, he focused his spiritual senses through his arm and hand, seeking the threads of life force and spirit that bound Domar's essence to his body. The threads were weak and frayed, his spirit eroded and his life drained. Even so, Ask could sense no sickness, no parasite or malevolent spirit poisoning the man's life. Ask knew his skill at sensing and detecting spiritual energies was deficient, but for a case as severe as this even he should have been able to feel something.

Ask opened his eyes. The hand that had been covering his nose and mouth dropped to his side to fumble with one of his belt pouches. He cast a glance back toward the door. Isond and Bergr stood just beyond the entryway, watching him, trepidation written plain across their features. Beyond them, Ask could see Haering facing in the opposite direction, his axe resting on its head beside him, handle held loosely in one hand as he stood on guard.

'Come,' Ask said. 'It's safe enough.'

Reacting almost immediately to his words, Isond strode swiftly through the entry and past Ask, dropping to her knees between Domar and the fire pit. 'What can I do, houngan?'

'Snowmelt. Start up a fire. Get me some clean cloth. Check if the others are still alive.'

Bergr was more cautious, nervously inching his way forward as Ask gave his instructions to Isond. 'Dauðvís' blackened bollocks,' he whispered, his voice hoarse, when he saw the condition Domar was in.

'Make yourself useful,' Isond said. She was already standing up, thrusting a cast-iron pot toward the warrior. 'Fill this with clean snow and get me some kindling while I check his family.'

Bergr took the pot and nodded dumbly, turning and leaving the house at ten times the speed he had entered it.

Ask found what he was looking for in his belt, a small white cloth stitched with the veve of Hvítr Løgursdóttir. He used both hands to unfold it and spread it over Domar's chest. The symbol of purity and healing would help to focus Ask as he tried to determine the nature of the affliction. He moved with practiced ease; this was something he had experience with. He was a healer, here was his patient.

'They are alive, Luta and the two boys. The girl, the youngest, is not here. They are all the same. What is wrong with them? Is it…a plague?' asked Isond, her voice low and tinged with anxiety.

'No,' said Ask, irritated. He would not have told them it was safe to come inside if he had thought it might not be. Isond should know that. 'I am not sure what is wrong with them. I do not sense any sickness.'

'Of course they are sick. Look at them.'

'It could be poison,' he said, more to himself than to Isond. 'Venoms are harder to detect, and their symptoms are similar to some spider or millipede bites.'

Isond stood abruptly, casting her eyes about the floor, suddenly excessively cautious regarding anything that might be crawling around. Bergr chose that moment to return, Eydis beside him with the pot full of snow. Isond's obvious disquiet made him hesitate at the threshold. 'Is everything...? How are they?'

'Alive, for now,' responded Ask. 'I need that snowmelt.'

The reminder seemed to jolt Isond out of her wariness. She gestured for Bergr and her mother to bring the materials they'd gathered over to her. She set about starting a small fire using the tinder, setting the pot down beside the fire pit. Eydis hunched over beside her to help where she could, tossing her long braid over her shoulder out of the way. Bergr gingerly stepped over to stand beside Ask. Isond worked on the fire until it had caught and grown to a useful size, then her mother carefully held the pot of snow over the flames until it melted.

Isond dipped a length of grey cloth into the still-cold water, wrung it out then handed it to Ask. He wiped the clamminess from Domar's face and neck then held it back out toward her. 'Another,' he said.

She obliged him, taking back the used cloth to be cleaned in the pot and handing him a fresh one. This one, he rolled into a cylinder and tucked into his fist, his free hand returning to Domar's chest with the runic veve between his palm and the man's flesh. Holding the cloth over the back of his hand, Ask squeezed it. A short stream of water splattered against his skin, trickling down between his fingers and into the white cloth.

'*Vatn Hvítr Løgursdóttir, mwen bezwen bon konprann ou,*' he muttered under his breath as he worked, concentrating on feeling for Domar's life force much as he had earlier. '*Ede m 'wè maladi a.*'

The invocation focused his spirit, sharpening his senses and making it easier for him to feel around for the malady that had overcome the man. There was a trace of something, some sort of malignant energy lingering in his body that Ask hadn't been able to sense before, but it was faint, its source long since gone. It confirmed that this was the work of a malign spirit, but Ask couldn't tell anything more than that. There was no evidence of sickness or plague but for the outward symptoms. Nor were there signs of damage caused by a poison or venom. Domar's body was simply not working, dying as it failed to distribute the nutrients it needed, slowly shutting down as his flesh starved.

Ask opened his eyes and withdrew his hand, his expression pensive. His mind worked furiously, thinking back to everything he had ever been taught about frailties of the flesh. After a few moments of contemplation, he again reached for his belt, this time unsheathing the small knife he wore there. He took up Domar's limp wrist in his free hand.

'What are you…?' Isond started to ask as the blade of the knife slid across the meat of the man's arm, cutting shallowly into his flesh. Ask flipped the knife in his hand and offered it, handle-first, to her and she quieted, taking the knife from him without another word. Domar wasn't bleeding.

Ask squeezed the cut, massaging it to encourage the flow. Thick blood eventually started to ooze out, so dark it was almost black.

'What is wrong with him?' Eydis asked.

Ask didn't reply straight away. He wiped some of Domar's blood onto his finger and brought it close to his face so he could look at it more closely. He sniffed at it, then tentatively touched it with his tongue. He looked back at Domar. The wound had stopped weeping blood almost as soon as Ask had relieved the pressure on it. 'It is his blood,' he said, finally. 'He has lost a massive amount, somehow. There is barely any in his veins.'

'But that...they do not have any wounds,' blurted Isond. 'That cannot be, I mean, we would see it. Would we not?' She looked over her shoulder, her gaze lingering on each of the other near-corpses.

'Strip him,' ordered Ask, rising to his feet. 'Take his clothes, clean off the filth. I need to take a closer look at him. Keep him warm.'

Without waiting to see who was following his instructions, he turned and walked back outside. The others had brought the wagon up alongside the house, the horses reins tied to a post hammered into the ground for that purpose. Haering stood nearby, looking toward the tree line. His adopted father glanced over when Ask approached. 'Houngan,' he said.

Ask gave a distracted nod in response and made his way over to the back of the wagon. Haering turned back away.

Ask rummaged through the contents of the wagonbed, stopping a few moments later when he realised he had no idea what he was looking for. Resting his hands on the coarse wood, he let his shoulders and head sag. There wasn't very much they could do for Domar or his family except care for them. Though they didn't seem to be in any immediate danger of dying, only time would tell whether their bodies would recover properly from the ordeal they'd been through.

Several long minutes dragged by. Eventually, he grabbed their satchel of provisions and slung it over his shoulder before filling his hands with a pair of waterskins. As he walked back over toward the house, he stopped by Haering's shoulder. 'Everything quiet?'

Haering nodded slowly, still watching the trees. 'The woods are holding their breath. Something bad happened here,' he said. After a moment, he turned to look at Ask. 'Is there anything you would have me do, houngan?'

'I think we will be resting here tonight,' Ask said. 'Could I ask that you see to the horses?'

'Of course, houngan,' Haering said.

Ask noted that the warrior's voice held none of the trepidation and anxiety he had heard in the others. He glanced over toward the barn. 'The daughter is missing; she might be in the barn. The animals...I do not know how long Domar and his family have been like this. If the livestock have been starved, this could easily ruin their entire livelihood. The others are helping me inside, but I will get Bergr to come out and go with you.'

Haering shook his head. 'Not necessary, houngan. I can take care of myself. If I need aid I will call for it.'

'All right. Shout if you find anything.'

The warrior inclined his head, picking his axe up and resting it casually against his shoulder as he turned and started moving toward the barn. Ask stood for a moment and watched him leave, envying the warrior's composure. Haering was a rock—nothing seemed to faze him until he was actually in combat and the battle-lust descended. Ask felt that he was lucky to have been raised by such a man.

Ask took a deep breath to steady himself, trying to mimic the other man's nonchalance, before he walked back into the house. Inside, Eydis knelt over Domar, part-way through washing the filth from him. Domar's clothes were in a bundle near the door, leaving him nude apart from the remaining waste. Isond was seeing to Domar's wife, Luta, with Bergr's assistance. Bergr's nose was crinkled in distaste, their task evidently unpleasant enough for him to at least temporarily forget his unease.

'I think we have found something,' Eydis said as Ask knelt down opposite him. 'Look here.'

Half-buried under body hair, there was a pattern of ugly purple and red welts tracing a small path from the corner of Domar's crotch to his hip, on the left side of his body. A tiny spot of dried blood tipped each mark, lending them the appearance of bites from a large insect. Ask placed the waterskins down beside him and unshouldered the food satchel, reaching down to touch one of the bites. He found the skin unyielding, the flesh beneath swollen and inflamed.

'Over here, as well,' called Isond.

Ask looked up at Eydis. 'We need to get water into them, and some food if we can.' He gestured to the satchel and skins he had brought back in with him. 'He might be too weak to chew. Soak the bread in water until it is soft enough that he does not need to.'

His instructions delivered, Ask stood back up and walked over to Isond and crouched down next to her. Sure enough, there was a matching set of bites across Luta's stomach, tracing an arc around her belly button to just under her right breast. 'They look like insect bites?' Her tone turned the statement into a question.

'I have not seen any insects that could leave a mark like this,' Ask said quietly, kneeling down beside her to examine the bites on Luta. Without a thick carpet of body hair to conceal them as there was on her husband, the marks showed up vividly on Luta's sun-darkened skin. 'They look far more inflamed than I would expect, and look how distinct they are even now. These people have been here for two or three days, at a guess. The bites should have faded by now.'

'What, then?'

'There are a few evil spirits that feed on blood. Parasites that drain people of their vitality,' he said. 'I do not know enough to be able to say what we might be dealing with. Houngan Igul would know. We need to find him.' Ask rose to his feet, trying to channel Haering's composure and Lorajaðr's confidence. 'We will have to stay here tonight and take care of Domar and his family. Haering is on watch for now; Bergr will take over when we are bedding down for the evening.

'Everyone else takes a turn on watch after that.' Ask hesitated for a moment, looking around at the others. 'Stay vigilant. If you need to relieve yourself, someone else should go with you. I do not think it is a good idea for anyone to be alone at the moment.'

- - -

A hand on Ask's shoulder stirred him from a restless sleep. He blinked blearily, looking up at the shadowy figure.

The door of the house was ajar, letting a gentle stream of moonlight splash across the floor and outlining Isond as she knelt over him. 'Your watch,' she said, her voice a whisper.

Ask pulled himself to his feet and made his way toward the door, his jaw cracking in a yawn as he carefully navigated the scattered lumps of sleeping bodies. Stepping out into the cool night air, he was surprised to find Isond a step behind him. She pushed the door closed behind her and they stood there quietly for a moment. 'Everything quiet?' ventured Ask.

'Quiet enough.'

One of the horses whickered softly next to them. Ask ignored it, slowly walking past to the unhitched wagon that had been left up against the side of the house. He looked out towards the forest they had come through on their way in. The trees stood quiet watch over the snow, unmoving and impassive in the pale moonlight. A small cluster of fireflies weaved and bobbed through the air at the far end of the well-trodden path, in the direction of Engerdal. An owl hooted somewhere off in the darkness.

Ask leant back against the wagon, another yawn struggling free of his lips. Isond followed, standing a couple of paces to his left. 'You can go rest now,' said Ask. 'I am on watch until morning.'

He wasn't sure what it was, but there was something off about the scene, making him uneasy. The fireflies, perhaps. It was unusual to see them at this time of year. Normally they would hibernate as larvae during the winter months.

'I know.' Isond leant against the wagon next to him, facing out into the darkness. 'I just…something feels wrong.'

'Feels wrong?' Ask feigned nonchalance, trying not to give away his own unease.

'This entire time, I felt it. Like I was being watched,' she said.

'We are all on edge. I was not sure what we were getting into, coming here, but none of us were expecting what we found. It is normal to be unsettled.'

Isond shook her head. 'It is not that. I have been hunter and prey enough times to know what it feels like to be watched, and I feel it right now.'

Ask was silent for a few long moments, wrestling with his own feelings. 'Give me a moment,' he said. If he gave voice to his own concerns, it might make Isond feel worse. Even so, they both felt that something was wrong. It was worth checking, at least.

Taking a step toward the tree line, Ask closed his eyes and took a deep breath, focusing himself. After a moment, he cast out his senses, feeling for any nearby presences. This was one of his weakest areas of expertise, as far as spiritual power was concerned. Fulnir had always displayed a much more solid grasp of this technique, being able to notice and even identify nearby presences quicker and more accurately than Ask had ever been able to.

A slight flicker of power brushed his attention, something so small he almost didn't notice it. He concentrated on it, trying to will it into focus. There was definitely something there, but it was too far away and he was too unskilled to tell much of anything about it. There was a feeling of malevolent intent, but it remained at a distance, hanging back so as to remain unseen and unfelt.

'There is something out there,' he said. 'I can sense it, barely.'

Isond stepped forward to join him, her gazing fixed on a point somewhere off into the darkness. 'Where?' she asked in a low voice. The sudden tension in her tone was almost palpable.

'Towards Engerdal,' Ask said, gesturing in the direction of the village. 'It is staying back for now, watching us.' He sighed. 'It looks as though our detour to avoid notice was a waste of time.'

They stood silently for a few moments, both straining their eyes to see if they could catch some glimpse of movement in the darkness. Fireflies bobbed lazily between the trees, tiny pinpoints of yellow dancing in the gloom. The sky had started to lighten slightly, the night having passed its zenith.

'It is cold tonight. You are not wearing your cloak?' Isond shivered, pulling her own closer around herself.

Ask snorted softly and looked over at her. He reached out a hand toward her then stopped, waiting. After a moment, she withdrew a hand from her cloak and tentatively touched his fingers.

She blinked, then grabbed his hand in both of hers. 'You are so warm!'

'Hyrr Lorajaðr is the master of my head, I warm myself with his fire.' Ask shook his head. 'It comes so easily that I do it without thinking. Foolish of me.'

Taking his hand back from Isond, Ask let go of the heat. He gave a quiet gasp as the cold air touched his skin. With the minor magic gone, he would cool rapidly now. '*Monskellr* sense magic just as we can. Even the small trickle I was using might have given us away. Stupid, stupid.'

Isond turned back toward the trees. 'I wish Fulnir were able to do that. His fingers can be like icicles.'

'He can,' Ask said, letting himself smile. 'It would be a bit more of an effort for him, as his patron, Vatn Luren, is of the water Lesir. The Hyrr are embodiments of fire, warmth is child's play for them. Fulnir has other talents.'

The silence returned, their conversation trailing off. Ask rubbed his forearms. Isond was right, it was cold tonight. He would have to head back inside to get his cloak.

'Do you think Houngan Igul and Fulnir are alive?' Isond said.

'I do not know.' Ask sighed again. He had been wrestling with that thought himself, wondering if they were wasting time here when they should be heading onward more quickly. 'Houngan Igul is strong and wise. If anyone could dispel the evil that has taken root here, he could. Fulnir is near enough to being a full houngan in his own right. You know how clever and capable he is. Together, they are formidable. But anyone can be caught off-guard or ambushed, and we have heard nothing from them for days. Either they are dead or disabled and unable to send for help, or Houngan Igul has determined that it is unsafe to try to communicate.'

'Or they tried to reach us and were stopped, somehow,' Isond said. 'Messengers can be intercepted.'

'Or that,' Ask acknowledged.

'And the rest of Engerdal?'

He didn't respond immediately, weighing each word carefully before speaking. 'I fear the worst. The omens have been bad.'

Isond turned her head to glance back at the house. 'This farm is one of the furthest from the village proper. I would reckon that Domar and his family would either be some of the first people to be attacked or the last. But…they have been invalid for days. A whole family, not being seen by anyone for that long? In winter, when it is not expected that they would be working their fields? Someone would have noticed, or come to visit. It does not look as though anyone has.'

'It does not bode well,' Ask agreed.

They stood in silence for a few moments.

'I am still not used to it,' Isond said suddenly, turning her head to glance sidelong at him. 'You being a houngan. I mean, I knew it would happen eventually. Fulnir as well. It is just...I look at you and I can still see the reckless little boy that thought it would be a grand prank to let Solveig Galinsson's chickens out of their coop and lure them into his house while he was passed out after Jarlsday.'

Ask smiled at the memory. 'It was supposed to be funny, with him waking up covered in feathers and droppings. I was eleven. How was I supposed to know that alcohol can kill birds?'

'You were so reckless as a child. Sometimes I wonder what happened to change that.' She grinned and shook her head. 'Your da really let you have it for that one?'

'I deserved it. It hurt to sit down for a week.'

'But that did not stop you the next time, did it?'

'Not at all,' Ask said, but his smile had vanished. It had been a while since anyone had last brought up his parents. He let out a long sigh, turning back to look out into the darkened woods beyond the farmstead.

'Are you all right?' The humour had gone from Isond's voice, replaced with a mild tone of concern.

'I am fine,' Ask said. 'It has just been a while since I thought about them.'

'Sorry.'

'Do not be. It was a long time ago, now.' He leant back against the wagon again, facing her. 'Want to know a secret?'

'Oh?'

'I am not used to it yet, either. The way everyone speaks to me now—I expected it, I suppose, but I do not feel any different. I thought when I became a houngan I would be surer of myself, that I would always know what to do. It is not that simple, though,' he confessed. 'Everyone is looking to me for guidance, but I am constantly worried that I am making the wrong decisions.'

'You have managed well enough so far,' she said. 'Houngan Igul thinks you are ready. Jarl Løgur thinks you are ready. Just trust your instincts. Go with your gut.'

Ask was silent for a few moments. Isond was right. He shouldn't be second-guessing himself so much. Right now, his gut was telling him that they were idly wasting their time here while something terrible watched and waited for them in Engerdal. Isond had said that it was likely that this family had been the last to have been affected—what did that mean, then, for the other Engermen?

Domar and Luta would live, once they had time to recover, but it was likely there would be others. If they were too far gone to help tomorrow, would it have been Ask delaying that killed them? Houngans and mambos were supposed to be decisive; others looked to them for firm guidance and leadership. Meanwhile, Ask was hanging back, taking things slow and careful, scared that he might mess things up or make the situation worse. What decision would Igul make in his place?

'Rouse the others.'

Isond looked at him curiously. 'It will be dark for a while yet.'

He shook his head, taking his back off the wagon and turning to face her. 'We are rested enough. Whatever is out there, it is happy to sit back and watch us. I do not want it to be happy. I want it to be worried. I want it to be scared. I thought we could sneak up on the village. I was wrong. I think it knows we are coming,' he said. 'The longer we stay here, the more time it has to prepare for our arrival. People could be dying while we sleep.

'We need to go in as quickly as we can. Save who can be saved. Kill what needs to be killed. Whatever evil has overtaken Engerdal, it has had time enough to grow fat and contented. No longer. We will find it, and we will destroy it.'

- - -

They entered Engerdal as the morning sun crested the horizon, shafts of crisp light filtering through the trees to spatter across the houses. At Ask's direction, Eydis drove the wagon slowly through the middle of the village. Silence bore down on them, oppressive and all-consuming. No Engermen came from their homes to witness their arrival. No fowl raised their voices to greet the dawn. Even in winter, there should have been people and animals everywhere, beginning their morning routines. Snowdrifts banked up against doors undisturbed, with no paths cleared through the village square.

The horses seemed unnerved, whickering constantly. Once Eydis brought them to a stop Isond took a moment to pat their noses and whisper gentle reassurances. Ask stepped down from the wagon and looked over the houses, turning slowly on the spot to take in the whole village.

Haering passed him down a spear from the wagon as the others armed themselves. Ask planted the butt on the ground like a staff, closing his eyes and taking a deep breath. Casting his senses out, he immediately felt something similar to the presence that had watched them at the farm, but the energy felt diffuse, spread out. He couldn't get an accurate feel of what direction it lay in, sensing it weakly all around them.

Ask opened his eyes to see Isond looking at him expectantly. 'The spirit's presence is clouded. I think it might be hiding itself from me, somehow,' he said. There were spirits that could confuse the senses, but Ask couldn't think of any that also drained the blood of victims. 'Split up and look around, see if there are people in the houses that need help. Isond, go with your mother and Bergr. Haering, with me. Call out if you find anything.'

The dug-in homes of the Engermen were fewer and clustered more tightly together than those of Innset; a mere dozen buildings crowded around the flat area that served as the village's gathering place. The thatch roofs were heavily laden with snow, several nights' worth at least, with no sign of any disturbance. The whole village seemed to be on the verge of being buried entirely, abandoned and eerily quiet as Ask and Haering moved cautiously toward one of the houses.

Haering used one booted foot to kick aside the snowdrift blocking the entryway and readied his axe, glancing toward Ask. They stood silently for a few seconds before Ask realised that the older warrior was looking for a signal to proceed. He nodded and Haering brusquely shouldered the door open, his body tense and alert for any sign of an impending attack. When none was forthcoming, he waved Ask over. 'More,' he said, gesturing to the bundles clustered around the fire pit inside.

'Help me check them, we need to know if they live.' Ask moved into the darkened hut, dropping his spear near the door as he began carefully rolling bundles over. The attention provoked a slow chorus of moans and groans. Two men and three women, in much the same state as Domar and his family had been; pale, weakened and feeble, barely able to move, much less communicate.

'Adal,' Haering said, his tone uncharacteristically soft as he placed one of his massive hands gently on the shoulder of one of the men. His eyes flicked up to meet Ask and he nodded toward the other occupants of the house in turn. 'Galin, Fastyi, Sigrun, Edda.'

'Family?'

Haering nodded and rose to his feet. 'Cousins. Adal, Galin and I share a greatfather. Fastyi and Sigrun are their wives, Edda is Fastyi's sister.'

With the two villages so close together, many Innsmen and Engermen were friends and even family to one another. Ask had been to Engerdal two dozen times or so before today, but his own family had no relatives here and with his studies, he was only really familiar with Houngan Hafgrim.

'I am sorry,' Ask said. He looked over the loose clump of bodies, wishing there was more he was able to do. 'We will do what we can for them, but we can ill afford to linger overlong.'

'As you say.'

At this point it was obvious that the whole village was suffering from the same affliction. There was still no sign of Igul or Fulnir. The images of battle that Hyrr Lorajaðr had shown Ask danced through his mind's eye, taunting him with promises of bloodshed and death.

Ask hesitated. The Engermen clearly needed help, but lingering might expose them to a trap or ambush from whatever had been preying on the villagers. Further, it was unclear as to whether Igul and Fulnir had even made it to the village. Ask prayed silently that staying a short while to care for the afflicted villagers was the right thing to do. He hoped that Hyrr Lorajaðr was feeling more benevolent than usual. His patron was a spirit of battle and violence and may feel that delaying here to help the sick was a sign of timidity or weakness on Ask's part.

Something about the scene before him caught Ask's attention. 'Haering, do your cousins have any children?'

'Yes, daughters and sons,' the warrior responded. His brow furrowed. 'None are here.'

Ask's train of thought was interrupted by a shout of alarm from somewhere outside the house. Ask turned to look toward Haering, but the bigger man was already headed out the door. Navigating the distance between him and the entryway in a few brisk steps, Ask scooped up his spear as he followed. Together, they rushed toward the source of the shout, weapons at the ready as they rounded a corner.

Bergr stood there, a look of sheepish embarrassment on his face as he wiped snow from his shoulders. Flakes of white dusted his hair and face.

'What are you playing at?' Isond said, a note of annoyance in her voice.

'Ah, my apologies, houngan,' Bergr bobbed his head awkwardly toward Ask as he patted at his head. 'A shelf of snow fell from the roof. It startled me, that is all.'

Ask turned his gaze from Bergr to the roof above him, slowly walking forward. There was indeed a chunk of snow missing from the edge of the roof, several feet from where the other man now stood. He stopped, narrowing his eyes. The remaining snow to either side didn't look unstable at all. The odds of a part of the shelf deciding to fall right when Bergr was walking underneath didn't seem that likely. 'Did you see anything?'

'No,' said Bergr, grimacing as he brushed a final flake from his ear and turned to look at the roof alongside Ask. 'Quiet here; might have been an ice fox?'

'Perhaps.'

Ask stepped past the house and looked toward the edge of the forest beyond. Turning slowly on his heel, he watched for any sign of movement or the shockingly blue eyes that would give away a fox. At the same time, he cast out his other senses, feeling for any malevolent presences. It was harder to focus when he was looking with his eyes as well at the best of times. The diffuse ripples of evil that permeated the village muddled and confused his senses, making it even more difficult to determine if anything else lay around them. After a minute, he turned back to the others, shaking his head.

'I believe it is safe for now, but stay vigilant,' Ask said. He used his spear to gesture to the houses. 'We check on the others, make sure everyone is still alive. Haering, Bergr, move anyone else you can find into your cousins' home and the one immediately next to it. Eydis, I want fires lit and stoked in those houses; we need to keep them warm. Then see if you can find any of their livestock and round them up. If any remain, they will need to be tended to. Isond, the people need water and food if they can stomach it. Take a look around the village and find what you can, but otherwise we will have to use the rest of our supplies. Boil some clean snow if you do not have enough water.'

'Yes, houngan,' came the chorus of replies, and the group was moving again.

Ask turned to look back at the tree line, his breath misting the air in front of him as his eyes probed the dark places between the naked birches. A nagging feeling of unseen eyes on him had lingered since Ask first felt the presence at Domar's farmstead and it made him uneasy. He still had no idea what it was they were dealing with.

Looking after the Engermen would hopefully serve as a distraction and relieve some tension; a concrete goal to replace the uncertainty they'd been faced with up until this point. For a moment, he almost felt calm. Focusing on the art of the healer for a while would be a welcome distraction from the sense of wrongness that pervaded the village.

- - -

A thin curl of white smoke wound its way into the sky above Houngan Hafgrim's hut. Ask watched it silently for a moment, weighing its meaning. The houngan's house lay to the east of Engerdal, a ways beyond the main cluster of homes. The smoke was thin enough that they hadn't noticed it until the hut itself came into view. Ask brought the group to a stop while they decided how to approach.

'Haering, Bergr,' Ask stepped forward, spear clutched tightly in one hand. 'Expect anything. We do not know who or what might lie within.'

To the side of the hut, a small fence of stone encircled what Ask knew to be a vegetable and herb patch, though a layer of snow buried all but the most stubborn of the plants. A great black crow sat on the fence, eyeing the three men as they approached. As they drew closer, it let out an ugly caw and took flight, wheeling in the air above them once before disappearing off into the trees.

Sparing one last glance at the warriors on either side of him, Ask raised his fist and pounded three times on the door. There was a moment of silence, then a faint shuffling sound from within. Ask waited, and the door shifted a crack. 'Igul, that you?' came a hoarse and weary voice.

'No, it is Ask,' he responded, relief seeping into his voice as a small smile curled the corners of his mouth.

Houngan Hafgrim pushed the door open until one tattooed cheek and a bleary brown eye could be seen. 'Oh. No. Not Igul,' he muttered, more to himself than anyone else. 'It is Ask. Houngan Ask now, is it not? Yes, Houngan Ask.'

'Hafgrim, are you well? Have you seen Igul?'

The older man laboriously pushed the door, leaning his shoulder against the wood and shifting it inch by inch. 'Well? Oh, no. Not at all,' he said. 'Inside, inside quickly.'

Ask looked over at Bergr and Haering. Hafgrim didn't seem his usual energetic self, and it would be disheartening for the others to see the powerful houngan at his weakest. He shook his head and gestured back toward where Eydis and Isond stood. 'I will take counsel with Houngan Hafgrim. Wait outside,' he said.

There was a dutiful 'yes, houngan' from the two warriors as he stepped inside and pulled the door firmly shut behind him with his free hand.

Hafgrim shuffled over toward the fire pit and let out a low sigh as he eased himself to the ground, giving Ask the opportunity to get a good look at him. The older man was pale, his wrinkled flesh sallow and sickly, much like the other Engermen. The only difference was that Hafgrim had enough strength to stand, though it was obvious that it was a near thing.

Ask felt a pang of sadness—Hafgrim had always been rather sprightly, wild and active, despite his advancing years. Even the unintentionally jagged tattoos that encircled his left eye and spiralled down to his cheek spoke of vigour and energy. Igul had told Ask and Fulnir once that Hafgrim was one of the more powerful houngans or mambos that he had ever known. Seeing him in this state was a sobering reminder of just how serious the situation had become.

The fire in the pit was low, almost spent. Ask found some kindling by the side of the door and knelt down to feed the flames as he spoke. 'We have been to the village. You look as bad as the others. Can you tell me what has happened?'

Hafgrim nodded wearily, his head and shoulders drooping with the effort. He licked his cracked lips. 'I was not strong enough to fight it. No, not at all.'

'Hold a moment,' interrupted Ask. 'Have you food, water?'

He shook his head. 'No. Gone, all gone. Did what I could for who I could. Too little, too little for everyone.'

Ask rose back to his feet and stepped toward the door, opening it and looking out toward the others. 'Was there any food or water left? Bring it.' Turning on his heel, he walked back over to Hafgrim and sat down across from him. 'You were expecting Igul? You have seen him, then?'

'Yes, they came three nights ago,' Hafgrim nodded to himself. 'Three nights. Back and forth, back and forth since then.'

Isond walked through the open door of the hut. 'Houngans,' she said, bowing her head as she entered. She walked up to them and knelt to hand Hafgrim an almost-empty gourd of water and a hunk of hard cheese. 'This is all we have left,' she said.

'Thank you, my dear.' Hafgrim dropped the cheese into his lap to hold the gourd with both hands as he took a trembling sip from its contents. 'This morning, that was when,' he said.

'This morning?'

'Yes, Igul and Fulnir, Fulnir and Igul. They left this morning, to end this. For good or ill.'

Isond looked up at him. 'They are alive and well, then? Houngan Igul and Fulnir?'

Ask cleared his throat to catch her attention. 'Isond. Go back outside.'

'But...'

'Isond,' Ask fixed her with a pointed look. 'I understand. I worry for them too. This is houngan business. I will join you all shortly and let you know what has happened.'

'I...yes, houngan. I apologise,' she said, frustration evident in her tone. She stood and retreated outside, pushing the door closed perhaps a touch too firmly behind her. Ask watched her go, a slight tinge of guilt tickling his stomach. Had he been too sharp with her?

73

Hafgrim raised the gourd again, letting the last of the water trickle between his lips before dropping the empty container to the ground in front of him. He sighed, rubbing at the dark purple bags under his eyes before speaking again. 'There is a cave to the north, by the river. We have had bears and foxes live there in the past. No trouble, no trouble at all until it moved in.'

'It?'

'An obia. Nasty one, too. I underestimated it. The thing killed a half-dozen good Engermen when we went after it, and I barely crawled away with my life.' He paused, leaning to one side to lift his tunic so Ask could see the rash of insect bites across his side. 'It changes into a swarm of locusts, crawls into the houses at night and gorges itself on blood.'

'An obia.' Ask felt a hard lump form in his stomach. 'I noticed that the children were missing. I should have realised. The blood threw me off. I did not think obias fed on blood.'

Hafgrim shook his head. 'They do not, normally,' he said. 'This one, though, it has worked out the knowing of evil, evil magics. It vomits up the blood in its cave, offers it up as a dark sacrament to the Faceless. It has kept me alive. Did not want to kill me, not yet. The blood of a houngan has power in it.'

'That would be what drew the tokoloshe Igul and I killed,' Ask said.

'Yes, yes. Igul mentioned something about that. There has been no sign of any other creatures of that kind near Engerdal. Likely a stray wandering the region that got attracted by the smell of the magic.'

'Where are Igul and Fulnir now?'

'They went to the cave. Yes, the cave. They fought it yesterday, the obia. Hurt it, but it hurt them too. They came back here to lick their wounds, then left again this morn to finish things. For good or ill.'

'This morning? How long have they been gone?'

'Too long, I fear.'

The lump in Ask's stomach moved up into his throat. He'd hoped he made the right call staying to help the villagers, but if they'd continued on to Hafgrim's hut more swiftly, they may have caught up to Igul and Fulnir. It was foolish to jump to conclusions, but Ask couldn't help but worry that perhaps the delay may have cost his old master and friend their lives. 'We leave immediately,' he said, trying to keep his voice firm. 'It may not be too late for us to help.'

'Yes. Yes, so you should, so you should,' said Hafgrim, nodding his head.

Ask rose to his feet. 'This cave, it is near to the river?'

'Go east from here, until you reach the river, then follow it north. You will come to the cave quickly enough if you travel closely along the bank.'

'We will return as soon as we are able. Pray for us,' said Ask.

'May the spirits watch over you, young houngan.'

Once outside, Ask took a deep breath and strode out to meet the others. Haering, standing watch over the trail they had come up to get here, turned his head to watch as he approached. Eydis still sat at the head of the wagon, her legs dangling down next to Bergr, who had found a knot of dead grass clear enough of snow to use as a seat. Isond had been pacing the length of the wagon, stopping once Ask emerged and taking an impatient step toward him before seeming to catch herself.

'We need to go, quickly. Tie the horses, leave the wagon. We will move quicker on foot,' Ask said. Isond opened her mouth, looking as though she were about to ask a question, so he held up a hand. 'Quickly now. I will explain on the way.'

Without waiting for any sort of response, Ask turned and started to walk east, circling around the low stone fence around Hafgrim's vegetable patch.

'Hyrr Lorajaðr Virdingsson,' Ask spoke quietly under his breath as the others hurried to gather weapons and follow him. 'With your strength aiding us, our victory will bring great honour and glory to your name.'

His grip on the haft of his spear tightened enough to whiten his knuckles. Hafgrim had said that the obia was already injured. With Hyrr Lorajaðr's blessing behind them, Ask was hopeful that it would be weakened enough for them to destroy without further bloodshed. However, with the fate of Igul and Fulnir still in question, his stomach twisted itself in knots.

Isond caught up, falling into step beside him. She was soon joined by Haering, on his right, Bergr and Eydis a step behind. Ask looked at Isond out of the corner of his eye. Her face was set in an expression of grim determination, a strung hunting bow held at the ready. With luck, the she would be reunited with Fulnir before the end of the day. Ask focused on that, using the hopeful promise of a reunion to distract himself from his fear that both Fulnir and Igul were already lying dead, drained of blood, at the bottom of the obia's cave.

- - -

The frozen surface of the river, its edges blurred and uncertain by snow and ice, wended its way beneath the overhang of the cave entrance. In summer, the water would flow into the cave, partially flooding it. A few feet beyond the entrance, the recesses of the cave were shrouded in what Ask imagined to be a solid cloak of darkness, impassive and foreboding, concealing whatever might lie within.

Ask crouched near a copse of naked birches a dozen yards from the entrance. The others clustered tightly around him, their muscles tense and senses alert to any sign of movement. The expanse of snow between them and the cave was churned and pockmarked, several reddish and dark stains marking the white, as though there had been a fight here within the last few hours. There was no sign of Igul or Fulnir, no bodies, nothing but eerie silence and the dark, forbidding mouth of the cave before them.

'Have a care,' Ask said, somewhat unnecessarily. 'We do not fully know what the *monskellr* is capable of.'

The others stayed silent, their eyes fixed on the cave before them, waiting for instruction. He took a deep breath and cautiously cast out his senses in the direction of the cave.

The diffuse presence he had felt in Engerdal itself was still present on the periphery of his perception—it had flowed and shifted some, but had not moved from the village proper to the south. Beyond that, Ask felt nothing. No signs of spiritual energies or life at all.

With no clear target, Ask felt his trepidation increase. The obia might be using magic he was not familiar with to mask its presence, or it may not be present at all. It might be outside of the cave, watching them and waiting until they entered before ensnaring them in a trap within.

He glanced at the others. Now would be the perfect time to ask the warriors for advice, but he could see the uncertainty and worry plainly painted on their faces. Even Haering's brow was furrowed in what Ask recognised as worry. If he didn't present a strong face for them, they would not go into this with courage in their hearts.

'We move as one to the entrance,' Ask said, fixing each of the others with what he hoped was a confident look.

Isond's lips pressed together in a tight line, her eyes narrow as she watched the cave entrance. Bergr appeared as nervous as Ask felt, his free hand worrying at the pendant he wore around his neck as his eyes flicked from Ask to the cave and back again. Eydis and Haering had both looked over when Ask had spoken and were now watching attentively, awaiting further instructions from the houngan. 'Bergr, you and Isond will stand guard just outside. If you see anything, call out. If I call out to you, come immediately. Haering, Eydis—you will accompany me. Be ready for a fight.'

Pausing a moment to ensure that everyone had heard and understood, Ask nodded once, then rose and moved cautiously toward the cave. His spear was at the ready, the haft held firmly in both hands with the tip pointing forward. The snow crunched softly beneath their feet as they made their way toward the cave. Ask's ears strained to catch anything that might be trying to mask its own movement with theirs, but he heard nothing over the pounding of his own blood. He moved his head slowly left and right, scanning the cave and its surrounds as he closed the distance.

Two-thirds of the way toward the cave, he paused. His companions froze immediately. Hunkering down, he took one hand off his weapon to touch one of the dark greyish streaks in the snow, then raised his fingers to his nostrils. The smell was oily, more like whale or seal fat than anything else. It reminded him of the blood of the tokoloshe they had killed, but many *monskellr* had similarly greasy bodily fluids. The breadth of his experience was too narrow to make any accurate determinations. He spent a moment focusing on the smell and look of the substance, fixing it in his mind so that it would be recognised if he were to encounter it again. Then he grasped his spear again and crept further toward the cave mouth.

The group stopped again, this time just outside of the entrance. Ask glanced toward Isond and Bergr, who nodded and took up positions near the side of the mouth, where they could watch the surroundings. It would be difficult for anything to sneak up on them from anywhere but inside the cave itself. Without a word, Ask walked slowly into the cave, flanked by the other two Innsmen.

At the entrance, the cave was wide enough to admit the three of them abreast, but it narrowed quickly until they were single file; Ask in the lead with Haering at the rear. Ask was forced to duck to pass through a bend in the passage. The stone walls seemed to press in around him as he made his way into the cave. Fifteen feet, then twenty, then twenty five and, suddenly, a solid bank of stone, creased and folded like old cloth. The weak light filtering in from the cave entrance was barely enough to see by, but directly in front of Ask, lay a family of white foxes, their eviscerated corpses dried and mummified by the cold.

Ask crouched to get a better look at the bodies. He could feel Eydis looking over his shoulder at the furry corpses and closed his eyes, casting out his senses.

'There is nothing here,' Haering said quietly, his voice echoing hollowly through their surroundings.

Ask held up a hand to quiet him while he concentrated, but he could tell that the older man was right. There was nothing in this cave. If it weren't for the family of dead foxes, Ask would have said there were no signs that a *monskellr* had ever been here in the first place. He rose to his feet and was just about to say as much when a shout of alarm echoed down through the cave from the entrance: Bergr's voice clear and panicked.

The three of them turned as one and started back, stumbling as they tried to rush over the uncertain footing of the cave floor. Ask's foot caught the corner of the bend in the passageway as he ducked down to pass through and he overbalanced, his left knee cracking hard against the rocky ground. A fierce jolt of pain shot up his leg. He ignored it, scrambling back to his feet as he continued through the widening cave toward the entrance. He reached the mouth of the cave in time to see Haering and Eydis start across the field of churned snow to where Isond was standing, arrow held nocked in her shortbow, almost half a dozen yards from where they'd left her. Bergr was nowhere in sight.

'Hold!' Isond shouted at as they approached.

A flurry of movement halted them before they'd made it to her position. Haering was dashed to the snow as though a great weight had suddenly struck him from above. He was wrenched to the left, tumbling a handful of paces before coming to rest in a bank of dirty snow.

Eydis recoiled the instant Haering had been hit. From Ask's position behind him, all that could been seen was a sudden, fine spray of blood from Eydis' shoulder and she was suddenly staggering back. Isond raised her bow, aiming directly for her mother, then let the arrow fly from her bow. It thunked home somewhere in mid-air, a scant foot from Eydis' head. Ask was close enough to hear a familiar, bestial snort of anger and pain.

'Tokoloshe!' Ask called at the top of his lungs as he flew past Eydis, his spear jabbing toward where the arrow had landed.

Something unseen scraped along the haft of his spear. The weapon was almost wrenched from his grasp as something struck a glancing blow to his forehead. Staggering, he wheeled around to swing the spear in a wide arc in the direction the creature had attacked from. The wooden haft whistled through empty air, narrowly missing Eydis. She scrambled to join Ask and her daughter in a tight circle facing outward, backs close enough together they were almost stepping on each other's heels.

Ask scanned the area in from of him. There was no sign of movement. The snow had already been churned and dirtied and it was impossible to tell where the tokoloshe that had attacked them might be. Out of the corner of his eye, he could see Isond to his left doing the same, another arrow at the ready. Three or four yards in front of him, not far from the uncertain edge of the icy river, Haering was pulling himself cautiously to his feet, axe still clutched in his right hand. His movements were slow and deliberate so as to better react to any further attack. A barely-noticeable wince pulled at the side of the warrior's face as he put weight on one of his legs, but other than that it seemed as though he had escaped relatively unscathed.

Seconds passed. The ragged, panicked breathing of Ask and his companions was the only sound to meet their strained ears. Ask risked a glance to his right. Eydis stood slightly off-centre, a spatter of blood painting her right shoulder where her thick fur coat had been slashed to ribbons. Past her, a crumpled shape in the snow that Ask had not seen earlier marked Bergr's presence.

'Bergr?'

'I think he lives,' Isond said, her voice low. 'One of them stumbled, wasted their surprise. His wound looked shallow. Hit his head when he went down.'

'Can you make them visible?' said Haering, still standing in place several yards away from them.

'I do not know how,' Ask admitted. Igul had wanted to leave fairly quickly after his raising, and hadn't had time to teach him. 'We will have to make do. How many are there?'

'Three,' said Isond. 'I think. Hard to count.'

'What do we do?' asked Eydis, her voice level.

'We need to get—' Ask was interrupted by a sickening crunch as something struck Haering's knee from the side. The warrior's leg bent at an odd angle from the impact. Haering gave a wordless shout of pain and anger and collapsed to the side. He somehow managed to keep his other leg under him as he swung his axe reactively in an arc toward the source of the attack. Midway through the swing, there was a bellow of pain and surprise. Oily, dark blood spattered across the snow.

Ask was already moving to assist the injured warrior. Breaking the circle, he thrust his spear toward a spot just behind where Haering's axe had struck. The tip of the weapon skipped shallowly across unseen flesh, but now Ask was close enough to see the heat haze-like blur as the creature moved. He brought up the haft of the spear, slamming it solidly against the barely-visible creature. It stumbled back and into Haering's fist. There was a meaty sound of impact as flesh slapped flesh, but the tokoloshe managed to avoid being caught between the two of them. It ducked below or around Ask's next follow-up attack. Ask wheeled about, spear up in a defensive posture as he stood over Haering, eyes searching for the tell-tale blur the creature caused when it moved.

His gaze was attracted by a flash of movement as Eydis and Isond engaged their own attackers. Eydis blocked an invisible downward swing with the haft of her axe and thrust it forward. Ask pictured the tokoloshe being knocked off balance as Eydis jabbed her weapon in a swift counterattack, but the blade kissed nothing but air.

Several feet away, Eydis' daughter took a stumbling step backwards, thrusting her bow in what seemed like a futile motion toward her attacker. A second later, she grasped the weapon in both hands and twisted it sideways, diving down and to the right. Ask could see the bowstring stretch taut as it caught an invisible limb. Isond wrenched it tightly backwards. Her foot found solid ground and she bounced upward on it and drove her other knee into what Ask imagined roughly correlated to where a kidney would be on a person.

His view of the others blurred and he brought up his spear to block, but the attack didn't come from in front. The blur vanished and there was a sudden pain in his side as razor-sharp claws grabbed a hold of him. The world lurched at an odd angle. Ask had a brief moment to puzzle over how the creature had moved so quickly before he landed hard in the snow. His breath burst from his lungs as lines of pain raked across his belly.

Ask's muscles seized up as he gasped for air, taking him out of the fight for a precious handful of seconds.

Where was his spear? He wasn't sure when he had lost it. His fingers slid along a solid surface of ice as he groped uselessly around him. Eydis cried out in pain. Ask craned his neck in time to see her crumple to the ground, a gout of bright red spraying from a gash cutting deep into her thigh.

'...*epi yo montre sa a verite a!*'

The three tokoloshe snapped into harsh focus, their green-black bodies starkly visible against the white of the snow and birch trees surrounding them. One appeared behind Isond. She turned just in time to avoid the brunt of its attack, its claws clipping the side of her head as she dived downward. One stood near where Eydis had fallen, slick red blood coating one of its hands up to the wrist. The last stood over Ask, reaching down to finish him off. It hesitated when it became visible, only for a second. It was long enough for Haering to bellow a war cry and bring his axe down on the back of the creature's neck, nearly decapitating it in a single blow.

The tokoloshe crumpled, its death spasms sending a gout of warm, oily blood splashing across Ask's face. The young houngan struggled to pull himself to his feet, rising in time to see the creature that had felled Eydis launching itself toward them. Haering half-lurched, half-hopped forward to meet the attack, unable to put any weight on his left leg as it flopped uselessly below the knee. He swung his axe wildly. The tokoloshe side-stepped, ducking low under Haering's backswing and planting its shoulder solidly in his stomach. It hefted the warrior into the air and sent him crashing down again.

A cracking sound split the air. Haering plunged through the icy surface of the river, disappearing into the inky black water beneath. Ask was close enough to feel a spray of water as the warrior splashed through. He threw himself on the tokoloshe before it had a chance to regain its balance. He punched at its face, pounding it again and again with his fists. Its claws raked his arms, pushing him away as it stumbled backwards under the reckless assault.

Its muscles went rigid as something exploded through the front of its chest, grey blood dribbling down its body. Ask paused long enough to see the metal tip of a spear retreat back through the creature's insides. The tokoloshe pitched forward, landing face-first in the snow in front of him to reveal its killer.

'Fulnir?' Ask said, wheezing out the name of his former fellow apprentice between ragged breaths.

The younger man's eyes were wide, his expression set somewhere between grim determination and terrified panic. Dried blood crusted his hair and clothes, both dark grey and rusty red. An ugly, puckering wound traced its way from his left cheek down to below the neckline of his torn tunic. Without pausing to acknowledge Ask, he spun on the spot and tore towards Isond and the final tokoloshe.

'Fulnir!' Isond had turned and saw the hounsis as he ran toward her. Her face lit up with excitement and surprise.

Taking advantage of the distraction, the tokoloshe dropped down low, swinging its arm toward her belly. She saw it move toward her and twisted, but she still caught the creature's forearm in her stomach hard enough to bend her over double. She dropped to the ground, winded, and the *monskellr* turned, loping off into the trees.

Fulnir ignored the creature, dropping to one knee next to Isond. Ask saw him roll her over and lean down to speak to her.

Ask spun back toward the hole in the ice, where Haering had disappeared a handful of seconds earlier. He yanked free the iron brooch holding his cloak in place and shook it free from his shoulders. Carefully, he took a few steps out onto the ice. Dropping to his hands and knees, he crawled out onto the river, testing his weight carefully as he scrambled up to the edge of the smashed ice. He glanced back toward the others. 'Fulnir!' The hounsis looked back up at him. 'Start a fire! Haering went under!'

With the ice and snow covering it, the water was almost impenetrably black, but Ask thought he caught a glimpse of a shadowy shape not far below the surface. Taking a deep breath, he plunged his hand into the water, reaching down to grab at it. The river was shockingly frigid. The cold penetrated straight to Ask's bones, his aches and bruises protested violently. His rapidly numbing fingers brushed something. Leaning down hard on the edge of the hole, he pressed his body against the ice to submerge his entire arm up to the shoulder in the frigid water and grabbed hold of what felt like a solid limb.

There was a sickening crack and the ice below him shuddered. Ask had just enough time to take a deep breath before the frozen surface of the lake fractured, plunging him head-first into the frigid waters. Even with a second of warning, the shock of being suddenly submerged knocked the air from Ask's lungs almost immediately. He found himself blind, his face stabbed by a hundred tiny needles of cold as the water forced its way into his eyes, nose and mouth. He struggled just to keep his grip on Haering.

The tumble had disoriented him, the cold muddling his senses. He started to panic. He couldn't tell which way was up. Reaching out with his free hand, he lashed about, flailing helplessly as he tried to find the ice above him. His fingertips brushed a solid barrier and he started to kick, desperate to reach the surface. Ask's hand pressed flat against the ice above him. He scrabbled at it, trying to find the hole he had fallen through. The strength in his legs waned as the cold leeched feeling from them., his frenzied efforts to escape only speeding the process.

His hand broke the surface, pushing through a muddle of icy fragments that had already begun to fuse back together. His fingers found the ragged edge of the hole, but he could not get a grip. His fingers slipped and slid as he tried to pull himself up. The edge of the hole crumbled. Ask clawed desperately at it, trying to will himself upward.

Something clamped around his wrist and dragged at him. Ask struggled feebly for a moment, instinctively trying to use it as leverage to pull himself up and out. His muscles seized up as the cold sapped the last of his reserves, but he felt his head suddenly break through the surface of the water. Opening his mouth to splutter and spit out water, he instead found himself choking as a fresh slurry of ice and water rushed in and poured down his throat. Hacking and coughing, he gasped mouthfuls of air between accidentally swallowing what felt like half the river.

Ask was wrenched out of the water, inch by agonising inch, and he found the water and ice replaced by thick, dirty snow. With a great effort, he turned and flopped onto his back, his lungs burning as he took great, gulping breaths. His arm was twisted at an awkward angle. Dimly he noted that his fingers were locked in a death grip that he did not seem to have the strength to break.

Air entered his lungs in short, sharp jolts, more like spasms than breathing. Shadowed silhouettes at the periphery of his vision wavered and solidified into a pair of figures on their knees, straining at something.

The young houngan felt the tension in his arm slowly relieve, then a second figure flopped onto the snow next to him. It took him a moment or two to realise that the others had managed to pull up Haering as well. There was sudden movement. Ask's blurred vision obscured any details, but he could hear Fulnir's voice. Something slapped his face, stinging his frozen cheek, and he tested his tongue and lips, trying to force out a word or two. Though his attempt at speech was unsuccessful, he felt oddly satisfied when he managed to make a low moaning sound. His lower jaw quivered involuntarily, sending a ringing sound vibrating through his skull as his teeth clacked violently together.

His arms moved without him telling them to and he found himself being dragged bodily through the snow. His surroundings blurred into a mess of shapes and colours, vibrant and out of place. As he blinked away the ice that was forming in the corners of his eyes he could make out something that he dimly recognised as an overhang of rock. The cave. There was a monster in the cave, wasn't there? An evil spirit? Ask could barely think straight, but he vaguely remembered something bad about the cave. He made a futile attempt to pull his arm back from whoever was dragging him so that he could crawl away from the cave. After a few seconds of straining he may have managed to twitch his fingers a little, but he wasn't sure.

A yellow light flickered into being on the edge of his vision and slowly began to grow. Ask's shoulder was moved roughly. Though he could barely feel it, he realised after a few moments of grabbing hands that his clothes were being peeled off of him. The light resolved into the familiar, crackling flames of a small fire, and his body curved reflexively, pulling him closer to the warmth. After a while feeling began to return, the warmth sending pinpricks of fire down his nerves as though his skin was burning.

He began to tremble, slowly at first but then more violently. A hand pushed at his shoulder, putting him flat on his back. His muscles screamed out in pain as someone started to massage the feeling back into them. Blinking furiously, Ask finally managed to focus his eyes and saw Fulnir over him, brow furrowed in concentration as he worked.

'…need you over here,' Ask heard Isond's voice. 'He's not breathing.'

Fulnir stood and stepped over the fire. Ask let his head loll backwards, resting it against the hard rock and closing his aching eyes. There was a shuffling sound, then a moment later he sensed someone over him again. A hand slapped his cheek gently.

'Hey,' Isond's voice floated down to him. 'Ask, hey. Come on.' His eye fluttered open again to see her kneeling over him much as Fulnir had been moments earlier. 'You need to stay awake,' she said, her tone gentle.

'Do not want…hurts,' Ask managed to mumble.

'I know. You are a fool, you know that? You could have died.'

Isond's hand was still resting on the side of Ask's face. He focused on that, using the contact to centre himself and push the ache of his muscles to the side. He still trembled, but the fire had started its work and the worst of the shivering had passed. 'S'my job,' he said. 'Houngan now. Got to protect everyone. Haering?'

She looked off to the side, back to where Ask assumed Fulnir and Haering were. 'He stopped breathing. I could not wake him.' Her shoulders sagged a little, a response to something Ask couldn't see. 'I am sorry.'

'Bergr? Your ma?'

'Both fine. Hurt, but resting.'

'Fulnir?'

'He is...' She looked back across the fire for a moment, then leaned in, lowering her voice so that only Ask would hear her. 'He is trying not to show it, but I can see he is hurting. Exhausted. It does not look as though he has slept. He has not said much.'

'Need to move. One got away. It will come back.'

Ask lifted his head, struggling to rise into a sitting position, but Isond put a hand firmly on his chest to hold him down. She shook her head. 'No. We are not going anywhere for a little while. You need to recover. Fulnir is taking care of the others, but they need to rest as well. We can stay here for now and move on in the morning.'

Sighing, Ask let himself relax and drop back to the ground. 'Cold,' he said. 'Tired.'

'I know. You need to warm up a bit before you sleep, though. Just keep talking to me.' She paused for a moment. 'Those *monskellr* that attacked us, they were not supposed to be there.'

'Tokoloshe. No.'

'Fulnir said the cave is safe. You did not find the spirit that Houngan Hafgrim spoke of?'

'No. Nothing here. I do not think there was ever anything here,' Ask said. His forehead creased. 'Fulnir. What did he say?'

'I told you, not much. He has not answered my questions.'

'Need to find out what has been going on. Head hurts. Cannot think.' Ask made a vague attempt at shaking his head and was rewarded by a stabbing pain. He let out a strained groan, the sound a mixture of pain and frustration.

'Tell me about them.'

'About what?'

'The tokoloshe,' Isond said. 'Tell me about them.'

Ask blinked a few times, recalling Igul's lessons and what he'd observed. 'Malicious spirits. Can vanish from sight by swallowing a mouthful of fresh water. Tricksters. Scavengers. They play pranks to start with. Tormenting people makes them stronger. They start to hurt people. They become more and more vicious, until people start dying. As weak as a child to start with, but can become much stronger than a man. Shorter, but with longer arms. Nasty claws.' He paused to yawn, his jaw cracking as his mouth stretched wide.

Time trickled by as they talked. Fulnir came over and checked on Ask once or twice, barely saying a word. At some point, once Ask was completely dry, Isond covered him with his red woollen cloak. He fell asleep soon afterward, his exhaustion proving too much to overcome for long.

- - -

Ask awoke to the touch of a gentle but insistent hand on his shoulder. Fulnir's voice floating down to him. 'Ask, wake up. We need to leave.'

Opening his eyes to see Fulnir's dark silhouette kneeling over him, Ask shifted his weight and let out a quiet groan. He reached up with one hand to rub at his eyes. His muscles were stiff and felt heavy as lead, every ache and hurt magnified. He could feel the stitches in his back tugging at his skin as he moved, parallel lines of dull pain running down the length of his back.

Fulnir grabbed his forearm and helped him up into a sitting position. 'It is time to go. We need to get back to Houngan Igul. He was not expecting me to be gone this long.'

The fire was out, though the outside of Ask's cloak was still warm, so it could not have been so for long. Only a subtle glow of predawn light suffused the air, just barely enough to see by. Ask could see Isond standing just inside the cave entrance, a half-dozen paces away, bow held loosely in one hand. She glanced over toward him and gave a tight smile, then resumed watching the darkened snow and trees outside. Bergr and Eydis leant against the hard rock of the cave wall nearby, just beyond the ashes of the dead fire. There was no sign of Haering's body.

'Igul is alive?' Ask tried to stand up, his knee flaring with a fresh bout of pain as he bent it beneath him. He grabbed at his woollen cloak with one hand, draping it roughly over his shoulders. Taking a moment to breath, Ask closed his eyes and carefully put his weight on his injured knee. It held, though it hurt badly.

'We were attacked. Ambushed. Igul was badly hurt. We barely managed to get safely away. We hid while we recovered.'

Ask nodded slowly as Fulnir spoke, wincing slightly as he took a couple of hobbling steps to where his clothes lay draped over a branch that had been placed near the fire. He paused and peered back toward Fulnir. 'What about Hafgrim?'

'He…I do not know,' said Fulnir, looking away. 'Houngan Igul thinks this is his doing.'

Ask didn't reply. Retrieving his clothes, he ran his hands over the material to gauge its condition. His tunic was dry but ripped, a gash torn into the stomach and a split down one shoulder. One leg of his trousers had been facing away from the fire and was still damp. His jacket was relatively undamaged, the leather slightly cracked and dry. He dressed himself, the task made difficult by his uncooperative knee.

Hafgrim was the one that had sent them here, right into an ambush with no trace of the *monskellr* he had claimed had taken up residence. Ask was hesitant to jump to conclusions, but it was possible that Hafgrim had lied to them and intentionally sent them into a trap. He needed to talk to Igul, work out what was going on.

Haering was dead. Ask stopped mid-motion, as he was pulling on his boots. His eyes burned and he took a deep, shuddering breath to steady himself. There was no time. Later, once they were safe, then he would be able to grieve properly. Until then, he had everyone else to think about. Breaking down into tears now might shake them. He would have to push through it.

Once Ask had finished readying himself, they left the cave. Fulnir led the way, the rest following in a tight group with Isond bringing up the rear. They circled around the cave and headed further north, following the river. The sky lightened as they moved, the sun slowly creeping above the trees to light their way. A light dusting of fresh snow had fallen during the night and the white powder crunched loudly beneath their boots as they moved. Everyone was alert, their eyes and ears sensitive to the smallest disturbances in their surroundings, fearful of another attack.

After an hour, Fulnir suddenly made a sharp turn to the west. Veering south, they continued on for ten minutes before Fulnir turned and started heading back toward the river. Less than two dozen yards later, he doubled back again and started moving southwest in a zigzag pattern. Another handful of minutes crawled by and Fulnir turned northwest, circling back in a wide arc. No one said anything, though Ask saw Bergr and Eydis exchange a look of concern. Turning around a tree they had already walked past several times, Fulnir seemed to vanish. Ask followed, the rest of the group close behind.

Impossibly, a healthy fire crackled in a dug-in firepit less than a half-dozen yards away, directly the middle of the path they had just walked through. Houngan Igul stood just beyond it, his staff held at the ready as he watched them approach. The old man visibly sagged in relief as Fulnir and Ask entered the area, then tensed and straightened up once again as the rest of the group followed.

'When I say to be gone no longer than a few hours, I expect to be obeyed,' Igul scolded Fulnir as they approached.

'I apologise, houngan. It could not be helped,' said Fulnir, his tone respectful.

'Igul, it is good to see you alive and well.' Ask felt his eyes burning again and swallowed the tears, forcing himself to smile instead. Though Fulnir had told him that his former master was still alive, the weight of worry in his stomach only dissipated now with Igul standing right in front of him.

'Alive, at least,' the old man replied, giving a tired smile in response. 'You took your time getting here, as well.'

A short time later, Ask was sitting beside Igul on a small log next to the fire. 'This campsite is impressive,' he said quietly.

The others were clustered on the other side, just out of earshot so long as the two houngans kept their voices low. Isond was replacing the blood-encrusted bandages binding her mother's thigh while Fulnir saw to Bergr's injuries.

Igul's staff lay beside him, his hand resting lightly on the unyielding wood. 'It is taxing to maintain, but with the tokoloshe stalking the forest it was the only way to stay relatively safe.'

'How many are there?'

Ask gingerly probed at his injured knee with his fingers. Nothing seemed broken or torn but if the stiffness and pain were anything to go by, he had at least bruised the ligaments.

'I am unsure. I have never heard of a bokor binding more than half a dozen spirits at a time, but we cannot afford to make any assumptions.'

Ask stopped and looked over at Igul, his eyes wide. 'A bokor?'

'Hafgrim,' Igul said. Ask could tell that the older man was making an effort to keep his tone relatively neutral, but there was still a ragged edge of emotion to his words. 'I know not how or why, but Hafgrim has betrayed the Lesir and the people of Engerdal. The plague that has struck them down is his doing.'

'Are you certain?'

'Do you think I would say it if I were not certain? Do you not think that I have searched for any other explanation?' Igul said, his voice tight.

'I am sorry. It is just...difficult to believe that Hafgrim would do something like this.'

Igul was silent for a few moments, staring into the fire. He had gripped his staff tightly with one hand, his knuckles turning white and trembling. 'I have known Hafgrim for over fifty years, ever since we were hounsis together under Ragnve. He is as a brother to me,' he said. 'I do not know how this could have happened. It does not make any sense. He was the most cautious houngan I have ever met. He never did anything that could put someone in danger without repeatedly checking he was doing the right thing.'

'When we visited him he seemed as affected as the other Engermen. It was an act?'

Igul nodded, his eyes still locked on the dancing flames in front of them. 'He never travelled, did you know that? We became houngans on the same day, after old Ragnve died. I could not wait to leave Engerdal, see as much of the Sundered Land as I could. Have adventures, raid the Jewelled Islands, perhaps become advisor to a jarl.

'Hafgrim, though, he stayed. He worried about what might happen to Engerdal if we both left. I had it in my head that we would be travelling together, so I tried to convince him. Mam Dagny was in Innset at the time with her three hounsis, and Mam Botvi had just settled down in Billingstad. They would look after Engerdal, I told him. He refused.'

'He was a good houngan,' Ask said quietly.

Igul laughed, a harsh and bitter sound. 'I was so angry, you know? I left like a child throwing a tantrum. Came back fifteen years later to apologise and he welcomed me with a smile and an embrace, then dragged me along with him. Gulbrand, Domar's father, had broken his arm the previous winter and his wife was with child, so they needed help foaling their mare.

'That was my welcome back to Engerdal. A decade and a half later and Hafgrim was the same as he had ever been. He always took his responsibilities so seriously. How could it be that he is bokor? I cannot understand it.'

'Perhaps there is an evil spirit befouling his mind,' Ask ventured.

'It is possible. There exist spirits powerful enough to force even a houngan into submission,' Igul said. 'I wish I could believe that that was the case. But spirits that strong are rare. Further, spirits capable of possessing people normally thrive on stealth and secrecy. Look at Engerdal— an entire village laid low, their lives syphoned away. There is no subtlety. No secrecy.'

'It could be something we have not heard of before.'

'Also true.' Igul paused a moment, then turned to look at him with red-rimmed eyes. 'What happens, then, if we assume Hafgrim is a victim? When more die or are hurt while we try to save him and he turns out to be beyond it? Whether because he is bokor or a spirit is wearing his dead flesh or whatever other reason. We must assume the worst, especially when all else we can grasp at are unlikely theories. We owe it to those already lost, and we owe it to those who require our aid and are clearly within our reach.'

'Because we are uncertain, we should cut our losses and give up on Hafgrim when there is chance he may be saved? I do not accept that.' Ask heard the note of anger in his tone, but he didn't know if it was Igul he was angry at or just the situation. Kald Jarl Løgur had told him that his tattoo marked him as a protector. Ask did not feel like he had lived up to what the Lesir had seen in him.

'You must, or more will die.' Igul rested his forehead in the palm of his hands, as though it were taking all of his strength to remain upright. 'How many tokoloshe were killed at the river?'

'Two. A third escaped,' Ask answered. 'I still cannot understand how he managed to bind so many spirits without us discovering it sooner. Even so, it has been less than a day since we were attacked. He will be weakened, with less servants bound to him. If…if we are to strike at him, we should do so quickly.'

'You may be right.' Igul gestured toward where the others were resting. 'But we are weakened as well. If we are killed, Hafgrim will be free to move on at his leisure. The Engermen live only because he needs their blood for his sacrifices to the spirits he has bound. If we die, he will suck them dry and then move on. While we remain here it is dangerous for him to move more openly.'

'I held counsel with Lorajaðr before leaving Innset. He foretold great danger, so I had Erlend send runners to Billingstad and Heggedal. If we die, others will come.'

'Then we should wait for them to come. Hafgrim is strong, you know this. As a bokor, he will be even stronger. I fought one before, a long time ago. It took seven to defeat him and two died to make it so.' Igul shook his head. 'We should wait and attack together.'

'What if you are wrong? Hafgrim knows we are hurt and in hiding. What if he decides to drain the Engermen to the last to replenish his magics, then leave? We can put a stop to him now, before he has the chance to do any further harm.'

Igul was silent for a moment. He looked older, somehow. 'We will most likely have a guarde to contend with—bokor bind them to their flesh. Do you recall?'

'I remember what you taught me. A guarde...the soul of a dead man, bound and driven mad? Like a pair of great, unseen hands that can cup around their master to protect him or be directed to crush and destroy. We will need to find and destroy the tattoo binding it to him. His cheek?'

'Unlikely,' Igul said. 'The binding is much easier if the tattoo is fresh. It will be hidden somewhere beneath his clothing.'

'He has at least one tokoloshe remaining.'

'I can teach you how to dismiss the shroud that allows them to move unseen. Is there anything else?'

Ask paused, thinking back on all that had occurred since they had reached Engerdal. 'There were marks on the Engermen, as though they were bitten by large insects. The village's children were all missing from the homes. We found no trace of them. When we spoke to Hafgrim, he told us that the village had been attacked by an obia, one that transformed into a swarm of locusts and crawled into their homes at night to drain them of their blood.'

'Missing children...there may be truth behind the lies. Hafgrim may have found an obia and bound it to his service, using it to collect the blood of the Engermen. We should be prepared to deal with one, if this is true.'

'An obia, a tokoloshe and a guarde.'

'And Hafgrim himself,' noted Igul. 'The bokor is more dangerous by far than the spirits that serve him. When should we leave?'

'How long would it take Hafgrim to bind more spirits to him?'

'A day, if there are any nearby he can find. Longer if there is not.'

'Tomorrow morning?' Ask said. He slowly flexed the aching muscles in his arm, resisting the urge to wince at the movement.

Igul nodded slowly. Ask thought he saw a bit more strength and confidence in his mentor's features than had been there before. 'Very well,' Igul said. 'We will rest until morning. Then, we attack.'

- - -

Ask breathed deeply, reaching within himself and drawing forth the energy he required. Slowly, he formed it into the pattern that Igul had taught him, turning it over and over again in his mind's eye, smoothing out the energy and fixing it firmly in place. The evocation was designed to rend apart the cloak that a tokoloshe wore to move unseen in the mortal world, cancelling its power out with a precise, opposing burst.

Paired with a prayer to Kald Sann Seithsdóttir, sister-in-law of Jarl Løgur and patron of true-seeing and justice, it was a powerful spell that would be effective even when used by a houngan with little spiritual power of his own. The Lesir had strong associations with certain domains and their name could be used as a focus to concentrate a houngan's strength and empower his magic.

'Houngan?'

Letting the energy he had gathered dissipate, Ask opened his eyes and turned his head to look at Bergr. He felt a twinge of annoyance at the interruption to his practice, but he was too tired to waste energy on caring overmuch.

Besides, he was fairly confident that he was able to shape the energies correctly. Bergr offered him a gourd and he accepted it with his free hand.

'Thank you,' Ask said, then raised it to his lips and took a generous swig. Slinging his asson back into its sheath at his belt, he swirled the gourd in his hand for a moment, feeling the liquid inside slosh about before passing it back.

'This is the last we have,' Bergr said. 'I thought we might as well put it to good use.'

Ask compressed his lips into a tight smile. 'How are you holding up?'

Bergr hesitated. 'In truth, houngan?' He paused to turn and glance toward the fire. 'Not well.'

Ask followed his gaze, looking toward the others. Igul hadn't moved from his place on the log for hours, staring into the flames and cradling his staff in his lap. Isond and Fulnir sat together on the far side from him, talking quietly. Eydis lay on her own a few paces from them, her back propped up against the trunk of a tree.

'I understand. Things were worse than we were expecting. I do not know if we will see another night after tonight.'

'Yes. No. That is not what I meant.'

'What did you mean?' Ask said, looking back toward him.

'When we were attacked, I failed to so much as injure one of the creatures. I was of no help.'

'That was hardly your fault,' Ask shook his head. 'We were ambushed, caught off guard. If anything you did well surviving the initial attack with no warning.'

'It was the same when we hunted the tokoloshe near home. I did nothing. You and Haering slew that beast. And this time Haering died because I could do nothing.'

Ask didn't know what to say, but he could not hesitate in responding, lest Bergr take his silence as confirmation of his fears. 'Listen to me. You are being unfair on yourself. These spirits are dangerous, difficult for a man to overcome. Tomorrow we go to fight Hafgrim and the rest of his thralls. With Haering gone, I need you to be strong. Look at them,' Ask said, flicking his head toward the fire. 'They are tired. Hurt. We all are. We need you more than ever.'

Bergr frowned, 'I…yes, houngan.'

Reaching out, Ask grabbed the pendant that hung around Bergr's neck and lifted it up, dangling it in front of the other man's face. 'You know what this is?'

'Of course, houngan. It is Lorajaðr Virdingsson's mark, a symbol of strength. It belonged to my father,' he said.

'Lorajaðr is your patron spirit, as he is mine,' Ask said. 'I spoke to him before we left to come here and asked that he guide us and lend us his strength. He watches over you even now. Do you doubt him?'

'No. No, I do not doubt him.'

'Your father, he was a great warrior was he not?'

'Y-yes, houngan,' Bergr stammered.

'This is his mark as well, so he also watches over you. Your father's guidance and Hyrr Lorajaðr's strength protect you. Would you shame them?'

'No, houngan,' Bergr looked down, avoiding Ask's gaze.

'Then you need to be strong. For Lorajaðr, for your father, for Haering and for the rest of us.'

'I...' Bergr stopped, then drew in a deep breath to steady himself. After a moment, he raised his eyes to look at Ask. His brow was set in determination. 'I will be strong. Thank you, houngan.'

'Good,' said Ask, giving what he hoped was an encouraging smile.

Bergr nodded and stepped away, walking back toward the others. Ask stood on his own for a few moments, thinking about their conversation. He was relieved and more than a little surprised that he had managed to allay Bergr's fears, but the other man's distress had only magnified his own concerns.

After a while, Ask walked over to where Igul sat by the fire. The old houngan didn't acknowledge him as he moved past, still staring pensively into the flames. Ask decided it best to leave him to his thoughts.

Instead, he circled around to where Eydis lay resting. She perked up at Ask's approach, using her hands to pull herself up straighter. A small grimace of pain shadowed her features for a moment before she gave Ask a bright smile—it seemed like the most genuine one Ask had seen since they'd arrived in Engerdal.

Ask returned the smile as best he could. The bandage on Eydis' leg was stained with a rust-red blotch that had soaked through; it was about time for the dressing to be changed again. 'How is your leg?' he asked gently, kneeling down beside the injured limb.

'Oh, about as well as you would expect,' Eydis said. 'Hurts like a bastard.'

Ask looked at her, taking note of the paleness of her skin and the clammy sheen that clung to it. 'You lost a lot of blood.'

'Not as much as the Engermen. I will not be doing any running about anytime soon, but I will live.'

'Let me take a look.'

Ask took his small knife from his belt and carefully cut away the blood-encrusted bandages. Fulnir had stitched the wound closed last night in the cave and the thick thread seemed to have held. Still, the wound had been deep. It would not have done Eydis any favours to be moved from the cave so quickly that morning. Ask retrieved a wooden bowl of snowmelt from near the fire and used the water to clean the wound before rebinding it with a fresh strip of cloth.

'What is our next move?'

Ask didn't answer right away, focusing on the task at hand. Once the wound was rebound, he looked up. 'We believe that Houngan Hafgrim is responsible for what has happened. We will go to him and put a stop to things.'

'Hafgrim, truly?' Eydis shook his head. 'I would never have thought...'

'Very rarely, a houngan turns from the Lesir and becomes bokor—a sorcerer. They make pacts with the Faceless and bind evil spirits to their service.'

'Bokor are very dangerous, then.' Eydis didn't frame it as a question.

'Yes.'

'Houngan, will you please do something for me?'

Ask nodded his head. 'Of course. What is it?'

She nodded toward the far side of the fire where her daughter sat with her lover. 'Take care of those two for me.'

Ask looked over toward the pair. Isond was talking quietly, her voice too low for Ask to make out. Next to her, Fulnir seemed less animated than Ask was used to seeing him. His head and shoulders drooped and he barely even glanced at Isond when he nodded or gave a short word or two in reply. Isond was smiling, but there was something about the curve of her mouth and the way her brow creased that gave away the concern she was feeling.

'I think they are more than capable of looking after themselves,' Ask said. 'Besides, once we deal with Hafgrim tomorrow, you can take care of them.'

Eydis' smile turned wistful and she looked back down at her leg for a moment before raising her eyes to meet Ask's gaze. 'I can barely walk. I will be no good to you in your fight tomorrow. Best to leave me here while the rest of you go on.'

'With no supplies and tokoloshe stalking the woods?' Ask shook his head. 'You may not be able to help us fight, but it will be much safer if we stick together.'

'I will only slow you down and make us easy pickings if something decides to go after me. I do not want any of you getting distracted trying to protect me when you should be focusing on putting down Hafgrim and his spirits.'

'No. You will come with us,' Ask said, his voice firm.

Eydis' smile faded. 'With all due respect, houngan, that is foolish. Having me there will just put the rest of you in more danger.'

Ask clambered forward, turning around to sit shoulder to shoulder with the older woman. He sat quietly for a few moments, composing his thoughts, before he spoke in a measured tone. 'Grein and Haering are dead. Killed by Hafgrim's damn spirits. That is *enough*. The Engermen lie in their village at Jarl Dauðvís' door, waiting for death, but we have not abandoned them and we will not abandon you either. We all survive. Together. I will be damned if I sacrifice you to protect my own hide. Do you really think me that cowardly?'

They sat there for a few minutes in silence, the crackling of the flames and the quiet murmuring of their companions filling the void in the conversation. After a while, Eydis sighed and gave a low chuckle. 'My apologies, houngan. I do not know what I was thinking. Maybe I am the fool, after all.'

'Damn right you are,' said Ask, letting himself smile. 'Now get some sleep. We will leave at first light.'

- - -

Hafgrim was definitely still in his home. Ask could sense his presence along with a hint of the clouded, confusing miasma of malevolent energy that clung to the rest of Engerdal. Part of him was surprised. Even if Hafgrim did intend to remain in the village for a time, surely it made more sense for him to move somewhere they wouldn't find him right away? If Ask were in his position, he imagined that he would have relocated to buy time to replenish his forces, in preparation for a sudden surprise strike against them.

He opened his eyes. The hut was just barely visible, tucked in amongst the trees ahead of them, its roof mostly obscured by a layer of fresh snowfall. Ask placed his hand on the trunk of a nearby birch to steady himself on the slope. They had circled around so as not to approach from the same direction they had left from, forcing them to move up a steep hill before turning to face their destination.

'I wish it were not winter,' Bergr whispered near to his ear. 'I would be a damn sight less nervous if we could set fire to the place and smoke him out.'

Eydis sat nearby, braced against a tree, Isond's bow in her hands and a half-dozen arrows stuck into the snow in front of her. One thing she had been right about last night was that she would not be much use in a fight. Still, she could at least watch for any danger approaching from behind. The short hunting bow she held could still be used reasonably well from a sitting position. Eydis gave a short nod of acknowledgement when Ask glanced in her direction.

Together, Bergr and Ask started to carefully pick their way down toward the hut. Igul had taken Isond and Fulnir and circled around in the other direction so that they could catch Hafgrim between them, attack from both sides. Right now, the others would be making their way closer to the stone wall that enclosed the vegetable patch on that side of the structure. Hopefully, one or two of Hafgrim's spirits would try to intercept them and they could destroy them before the bokor could join the fight.

Ask felt exposed. There could be a tokoloshe lurking anywhere nearby. Even approaching down a slope as they were, even under the moderate cover provided by the trees, they would have little warning of an impending attack beyond the signs of the creature's passage through the snow. They were hurt and uncertain of what to expect. If they were ambushed, it would only take a few minutes for them to be killed.

Ask's long knife hung in its sheath at his side and he found himself clenching and unclenching his fists nervously as he moved. Ask had made the decision to keep his hands free last night. He'd had some time to himself and used it to think about the defensive barrier he had created to shield himself from the first tokoloshe they had fought near Innset. Now that he had had a chance to think about the form his power should take and what the limits of it were, it would hopefully prove valuable should they be attacked by another of the spirits.

A flicker of movement in the corner of his eye caught Ask's attention. He paused mid-step and snapped his head around to look, his muscles suddenly tense. Had he really seen something or had it been a trick of the light? He strained his senses, both physical and spiritual, trying to detect any sign of movement from their flank. The encompassing miasma of power that clung to Engerdal still muddled the air, putting him further on edge. It may have been his imagination, but it seemed as though it was more focused, concentrated around Hafgrim's hut.

Ask swallowed hard, forcing himself to turn back toward their destination. If a tokoloshe was stalking them, they were as prepared for the inevitable surprise attack as they could be. He only hoped it targeted them rather than choosing to wait until they had passed and attacking Eydis. Ask didn't think Isond's mother would survive another such encounter in her present condition.

If it even was a tokoloshe. Hafgrim had lied about there being an obia at the cave, but that didn't mean there wasn't one at all. Ask's barrier blocked spiritual entities and should be able to protect against a guarde or obia equally well, but he'd prefer to test it under more controlled conditions before relying on it to save someone's life.

His thoughts were interrupted when he felt a short burst of energy emanate from the far side of the hut. Even from here, the power was recognisable as that which accompanied the evocation Igul had taught him that would expose a tokoloshe. A moment later, the magical energy was followed by a few short sounds of a struggle.

Capitalising on the distraction, Ask gestured to Bergr and the two of them loped swiftly down the slope until they reached the side of the building. By the time they got there, the sounds had ceased.

Ask paused, waiting for some reaction. From where he stood, he could peer around to the front of the hut, but the door did not open. A minute later, Fulnir's head popped out from the other side of the house. Ask raised a hand in greeting and Fulnir made a stabbing gesture in response. They'd killed something. It was a good assumption that the last remaining tokoloshe would not be causing them any further trouble. Ask was relieved that the creature had not had any time to build its strength.

It had seemed a fair guess that Hafgrim would come out to fight them as soon as he noticed their presence. The guarde spirit that they expected him to have was a much more dangerous opponent in an open area than within an enclosed space. Ask felt a touch of anxiety settle in his stomach. Hafgrim wasn't acting the way he had expected at all and it was putting him off-balance. Was there something they had missed, some further detail they had overlooked that would explain the bokor's actions?

Ask drew his long knife and, across from him, Fulnir did the same. The plan had been for the two of them to deal with the guarde spirit while Igul kept Hafgrim's attention off them. A shallow cut across the tattoo binding the spirit would be enough to break the magic that kept it anchored, followed by a short evocation to make the dead soul pass on. Getting close enough to the bokor was the difficult part, with the guarde protecting him and his own formidable skills to account for. The plan would remain the same. If anything, it'd be easier to get close to Hafgrim once they managed to force their way into the hut.

Ask started towards the door, keeping close to the wall of the hut as he moved with slow, careful steps. He had already formed the shape of the energy required for his barrier invocation, much improved now that he had had some time to mull it over and form a clearer picture in his mind for what he wished to accomplish.

The wall next to him exploded outward in a shower of splinters. Jagged slivers of wood stabbed into his left side and he staggered back. Something hard slammed into the side of Ask's head and sent him stumbling off to the side. He fell into the snow, his hands coming up reflexively to cover his face, his knife lost and forgotten. There was a sharp pain in his left eye and for a brief, panicky moment everything went black.

Struggling to right himself, Ask blinked rapidly and his vision cleared quickly. Scattered pinpricks of pain covered his left arm and the side of his face, but there wasn't a lot of blood. He recovered his wits just in time to see Hafgrim finish tearing his way through the wall of his hut.

The bokor's eyes flashed and glowed with a golden light, unlike anything Ask had seen before. Bergr struck at him with the haft of his axe, following it up with a powerful overhand swing. Hafgrim stepped back and let the axehead bury itself in the ragged edge of the hole he had torn in the hut. Then he sprang out and slammed the heel of his palm into Bergr's face. The much larger man was sent reeling backwards, losing his grip on his weapon.

Fulnir lunged at Hafgrim from behind with his knife. The bokor seemed to sense the attack coming, sidestepping easily and catching the younger man's wrist in one hand. He spun around, lifting Fulnir into the air and slamming him bodily into the wall. The wood shattered beneath the force of the blow.

Ask struggled to his feet, but Hafgrim was already advancing on Isond. She swung her weapon conservatively, using lighter, faster strikes to try to land a blow on the old man. He nimbly avoided each blow, somehow managing to dodge or sidestep each attack as he reached for her. Ask moved to try to intercept, though he had no idea what he could possibly do with no weapon.

Bergr suddenly streaked past, letting out a fierce shout of battle fury. The warrior scooped up his fallen axe and swung it in a wide arc toward the bokor's head. A stream of blood poured from the warrior's face and dribbled down his front, his nose broken from where Hafgrim had struck him moments earlier. Hafgrim ducked under Bergr's swing and took a step backwards, bringing his elbow into the warrior's stomach. The wind was knocked from Bergr's lungs. As Hafgrim went to grab hold of the helpless man's leg, Ask threw a punch toward the bokor's face. Hafgrim reversed his motion and spun away from Ask, narrowly avoiding the fist as he wrapped his arm backwards around Bergr's neck and used his momentum to knock the larger man from his feet.

Ask gaped. The bokor seemed impossibly fast and strong—how had he augmented his own physical abilities in such a way? Perhaps it was some variant on the guarde binding, fixing its power into your own limbs rather than allowing it to move independently? Ask wasn't sure. Whatever it was, they hadn't been prepared for it and he didn't know how to stop it.

Igul stepped past him, thrusting the butt of his staff like a spear. The hard wood slammed into the side of

Hafgrim's neck, just above the collarbone, with Igul's full strength behind it. The blow would have stunned or even killed a normal man, but Hafgrim only staggered back a pace or two, hate glimmering in his golden eyes. He snatched at the wooden shaft. Easily pulling the weapon from Igul's hands, he swung it in a short, sweeping arc that ended when the staff slammed into Isond's temple. She crumpled almost instantly, falling hard to the snow like a marionette with its strings cut.

Fulnir had managed to clamber free of the broken wooden debris and started to circle around, a thin, splintered log held at the ready in one hand. Igul moved in the opposite direction, putting Hafgrim directly between them as he unsheathed the long knife that he kept at his belt. Bergr managed to get his feet back underneath him, though he rested his weight oddly on one leg. The three of them formed a rough semi-circle around the bokor. As the others formed up, Ask saw an opportunity and used it to dart down past Igul, dropping to his knees and skidding as he came upon Isond. Grabbing her limp body under the shoulders, he hurried to drag her at least a handful of feet out of harm's way.

There was a thump and a surprised grunt of pain. Ask looked up to see the feathered end of an arrow that had sprouted from the space between Hafgrim's shoulder and his collarbone. He looked around and saw Eydis standing maybe twenty yards away, at the base of the slope leading to the house, back leant up against one of the trees. She nocked another arrow and drew back the bowstring, but Hafgrim didn't wait for the second shot. He bounded through the gap between Igul and Bergr, dodging their attacks, and interposed Bergr between himself and the archer.

In doing so, he allowed Bergr and Igul to draw dangerously close while flanking him from front and back. The two men took advantage of the misstep, coordinating their attacks. Bergr swung high while Igul stabbed low. The blade of the houngan's long knife bit deeply into the meat of Hafgrim's thigh. The bokor roared in pain and spun around to strike Igul across the face, sending him stumbling back. This gave Fulnir enough time to move into position to replace his mentor. He swung for Hafgrim's knee with a makeshift wooden club.

Hafgrim shied away, but Bergr shoved at his back with the haft of his axe, pushing him back into the path of the club. There was a sickening crack and Hafgrim's knee bent sideways, a splatter of red colouring the snow as bone splintered and poked through the skin. The bokor howled with rage as he toppled, using his good leg to launch himself on top of Fulnir. The two of them went down in a flailing pile of arms and legs, Hafgrim still shrieking as he beat at the younger man with his fists.

Bergr dropped his axe and wrapped his forearm around Hafgrim's neck, pulling him away from Fulnir and locking him in a hold. Fulnir did not rise again.

Igul buried his knife up to the hilt into the bokor's stomach. Hafgrim screamed and spat invectives in Igul's face. The houngan wrenched the blade upward, stabbing up under the bokor's ribcage, searching for the heart.

Hafgrim seized up, his whole body spasming, and then the bokor fell still, sagging in Bergr's arms. Igul kept his weight against the hilt of the knife for a few long seconds, grinding it up into Hafgrim's chest cavity, before releasing his grip on the blade and taking a step back. Bergr released his hold on the body, carefully kneeling down and laying the dead man on his back in the snow.

Ask walked over to Igul as he stood silently over the body of his friend. Igul looked up as the younger man approached, offering him a grim nod of acknowledgement. There was a tiredness to the old houngan's face that Ask hadn't seen before, an expression of grim resignation and acceptance.

Looking down at Hafgrim, the dead man's blank eyes staring sightlessly toward the sky, Ask felt a lump harden in his throat. Igul and Hafgrim had been friends for longer than Ask had been alive. There were no words of reassurance or commiseration that could be said that wouldn't feel hollow or ignorant, so he simply stood there, a quiet presence by Igul's shoulder, to at least let him know that he wasn't alone.

Igul knelt and reached out to touch Hafgrim's face, his fingertips gently tracing the jagged tattoos that marked the side of the other man's face. 'I am so sorry, old friend,' he said, his voice hoarse and low. 'You deserved better than this.'

Out of the corner of his eye, Ask saw Eydis laboriously moving toward them, leaning heavily against the wall of the hut to help support her weight once she reached it. Bergr caught Ask's gaze and gave him a questioning look, reaching out a hand to indicate Igul. Ask shook his head, flicking his chin toward where Fulnir and Isond lay near to each other in the snow. The warrior nodded in acknowledgement and moved to check on the pair, respectfully leaving Ask and Igul alone in their grief.

A long moment passed in silence. Ask barely moved, only shifting his weight to keep his injured knee relatively comfortable. There were rites and rituals they would need to perform to ensure Hafgrim's soul was kept safe from any dark spirits he had made bargains with, but Igul knew that and Ask wasn't about to try to tell his former mentor what needed to be done. Not yet, at least.

A great shudder passed through Hafgrim's body. Ask felt his muscles tense, his heartbeat suddenly accelerating as he took a step backwards and let out an involuntary yelp of alarm. Igul reacted faster, as though he had been expecting it. *'Lesir Kald bondye, pwoteje sèvitè ou kont sa ki mal sa a!'*

The spiritual barrier slammed into place as Hafgrim's body hacked up a spume of blood and spit in a great, wracking parody of a cough. A fat firefly, its abdomen swollen and luminescent, shot from the dead man's mouth and toward Igul. It slammed into the barrier with enough force to smash straight through, the magical energies coming apart as easily as they had come together.

The magic had, however, slowed the creature down. As it flew at Igul's face, the old houngan snatched it out of the air. He closed his fist around the *monskellr* and started to chant again. *'Hyrr Jarl Virding, mwen bezwen dife ou.'* Heat. Fire. Ask could feel the power Igul was summoning. He was planning on burning the *monskellr* alive. *'Se pou fòs kouraj ou ranpli m 'ak ban m' dife... ou...'* Igul stumbled over his words, his face twisting in pain.

Ask didn't see exactly what happened next. The firefly creature escaped from Igul's hand, somehow. There was a lot of blood—human blood—and then the old houngan stumbled and fell backwards, clawing at his mouth with both hands. Ask tried to help, but the insect had already forced its way between the older man's lips. Igul's eyes bulged in their sockets as the creature wormed its way down his throat. He started to thrash wildly around.

Bergr stepped toward them. 'What is it? What is happening?' The warrior's question was loud, almost a shout, and quavered with fear.

'Quiet!' Ask ordered. 'Stay back!' His tone felt surprisingly firm, considering that he felt as though he was about to start screaming.

The firefly. What was it? It wasn't something they had expected, and he didn't recognise it from Igul's teachings. Ask wracked his brains as he grabbed Igul's shoulders, trying to hold them steady as he desperately searched for anything, some scrap of knowledge he had been taught that might hold the key to stopping whatever was happening.

Igul's eyes had rolled back into his head. His entire body shook as though he was having some sort of seizure. 'Bergr, come!' Ask shouted. 'Hold him still!'

Bergr almost fell over skirting around Ask. He dropped to his knees and hesitated for a moment, trying to work out how to restrain the spasming houngan. Grabbing at the old man's shoulders, he pawed at him in a clumsy and somewhat futile attempt to restrict his movements. Releasing his own grip, Ask brought his hands up to cup Igul's face between his palms, trying to focus his mind on sensing what was happening to the old houngan.

The man's thrashing proved too distracting. Ask was having trouble concentrating. The threads of life force and spirit he was feeling for danced just outside his grasp. A small sound of panicked frustration came unbidden from the back of his throat. He took his hands away from Igul's head. Reaching into his belt pouch, he grabbed at the small cloth stitched with the veve of Hvítr Løgursdóttir and flung it onto the houngan's chest.

Pinning the cloth to Igul's body with the heel of his palm, he closed his eyes and invoked the power of the Lesir.

'*Vatn Hvítr Løgursdóttir, mwen bezwen bon konprann ou.*'

He could feel the old man's body spasming under his hand and pushed it from his mind, struggling to centre himself, sending his spiritual senses delving deep into Igul.

'*Ede m 'wè maladi a.*'

A crackle of white-hot pain surged up his arm, blasting through all of his senses and exploding through his head. Ask recoiled, his muscles seizing up and sending him crashing backwards.

'Houngan!'

Bergr's panicked voice came to him as though through a haze of sleet but he was helpless to reply. His body felt sluggish and unresponsive as he lay stunned in the snow. After a few moments, he managed to pull himself back up into a sitting position and promptly flopped forward onto his hands and knees.

'Houngan! Are you well?' Eydis lurched over to him, limping heavily as she tried to keep her weight off her injured leg.

Ask nodded, wincing at the stabbing pain that shot through his head with the motion. 'I am unhurt.' He looked down at Igul, still shuddering under Bergr's hands. The houngan's spasms had slowed somewhat. 'An evil spirit had taken control of Houngan Hafgrim,' he said. 'Igul fights it now.'

'What do we do?' Bergr asked.

Ask snorted in frustration and anger. 'There is little we can do. A spirit powerful enough to possess a houngan against his will is a formidable foe. The creature blocked me from lending Igul my aid…he must fight it on his own.'

'He will defeat it?'

The younger man could practically hear Igul's voice, repeating what he had said last night. If the old houngan had a say in the matter, he would tell Ask to kill him quickly, before the spirit had a chance to assert any control over him. However, now that Ask knew what to watch for, he could try to kill or trap the firefly creature when it tried to exit Igul's body. The fight would be over and Engerdal would be saved. If it managed to mount Igul, Ask wasn't sure the remaining Innsmen would be strong enough to defeat him. It would be a smarter move to put a stop to the creature before it could become a threat again. But then Igul would be dead. Ask wasn't ready to accept that.

'I do not know,' he said. 'Hafgrim was stronger than Igul, and the spirit overcame him. It may be weakened, though. The power it used while fighting us as Hafgrim may have drained its reserves. We need to prepare.'

'Prepare for what?' Eydis asked. The concern was plain in her tone.

'Ready your bow. If Igul loses to the creature, it will take control of him. I do not know what it is, but if it is stronger than Igul then none of us will be leaving here alive. It will kill us one by one.'

Bergr and Eydis did not reply.

Ask glanced over toward where Fulnir and Isond lay unconscious, then stood and took a few halting steps toward them. If he could wake Fulnir, between the two of them they might have a chance at breaking through and lending Igul their aid.

'Fulnir!' he called as he dropped down next to the young hounsis.

Heavy black and purple bruising was already starting to swell its way across Fulnir's face and neck from where Hafgrim had beaten him. Ask carefully touched his face with probing fingertips, checking his nose, cheekbones and jaw for any fractures. 'Wake up. Do you hear me? Wake up, you damn fool! I need your help! Fulnir!'

There was no response. Ask shot a nervous glance back over his shoulder toward the others. Igul was still writhing on the ground. Bergr had moved to support the houngan's head and neck. Eydis stood over them with an arrow nocked and ready to draw. There was a chance that the two of them would have enough spiritual strength to help him overcome the block. Bergr had no real training, but Eydis had experience in participating in the houngan's rituals. She would be quicker to focus and attain the necessary state of mind.

Ask had little else left in the way of options. Igul hadn't been strong or quick enough to stop the *monskellr* when it had emerged from Hafgrim. If the old houngan lost his spiritual struggle against it as well, the odds of Ask succeeding where he had failed were low. Even if they slew the person it was inside it would just take another, picking them off one-by-one until they were all dead. Every moment Ask wasted made it less likely that any of them would walk away from here.

A groan from beside him startled him out of his paralysis. 'Isond!' he said, his eyes flicking toward the other figure lying prone beside him. He shifted position so that he was leaning over her instead of Fulnir. 'Isond, can you hear me?'

'Ugh. Ask...What is—is everyone alright? What happened?'

'We were wrong,' he said, his tone urgent. 'Hafgrim was not a bokor. He was possessed by a *monskellr*. It is trying to take control of Igul.'

'What?' She jerked upright, reaching out to steady herself. Ask grabbed her hand, threading his free arm around her shoulders to support her. She squinted, wincing in pain. 'How... how can I help?'

Ask felt a smile of relief tug at the corners of his mouth, despite their situation. 'I need you and your mother both.' He helped her to her feet as he spoke, painfully putting more weight on his injured knee and together they half-stumbled, half-walked over to where Igul lay twitching. 'Eydis! Put up your bow.'

'What do you need, houngan?' Eydis asked, clearly relieved as she threw her arrow point-first into the snow and slung the bow over her shoulder.

'Kneel down next to him,' Ask instructed. 'You too, Isond. Get on either side of him. I am going to need both of you to lend me your strength to break through the barrier that the creature has erected. Clear your mind. Focus on Igul and I, just as you would when drumming during one of our rituals.'

Ask straddled the old man's torso. 'Bergr, have you a knife?' he asked. The warrior shook his head. 'Get one. Take the one stuck in Hafgrim if you have to. If I give the word, you must cut Igul's throat. No hesitation.'

'Y-yes, houngan,' Bergr said. The warrior's eyes were wide with fear.

He moved out from under Igul, letting the old houngan's head drop to the snow, and scrambled off to retrieve a knife. He returned a moment later, carefully looping one hand underneath Igul's chin to lift it, holding the blade to the houngan's throat with the other. The warrior's hands shook, but he kept them steady enough to not accidentally harm the old man as he leant down over him.

Taking a deep breath to try and calm the frenzied beating of his heart. Ask reached down and placed his palms against the sides of Igul's head and closed his eyes.

'*Kald Jarl Løgur, se pitit gason ou lan menase,*' he chanted. '*Hyrr Jarl Virding, mwen bezwen fòs ou an kounye a. Vatn Jarl Dauðvís, gadyen nan syèl la, sa a houngan se pa pare 'ale ak nou.*'

Unsure what was the most appropriate spirit to appeal to, he chose to invoke all three jarls—the heads of the most prominent families of Lesir. If he offended them by calling to them all at once, it was something he would gladly make up for later.

He could sense Isond and Eydis next to him, dully shining with energy in his mind's eye. They were already poised to add their strength to his own. A quiet, steady cadence reached Ask's ears. It took him a moment to realise that Eydis was drumming against the side of her leg with her palm, the rhythm recognisable as that belonging to Jarl Løgur. Ask felt a surge of confidence. They could really do this. Taking hold of their combined power, he wrapped himself in it and reached his spirit down into Igul, pressing up against the barrier that blocked his aid.

'*Gwo jarls, sa a houngan te gen yon sèvitè fidèl ak rete fidèl pou plizyè ane. Yon prezans nwa genyen batay l'*—'

Ask's spirit was thrust violently back into his own body. Igul shuddering beneath him. The surge of confidence crashed into a wave of despair. The fight was over. He had not been fast enough. Ask opened his mouth and eyes, about to give Bergr the order to kill the old houngan. He hesitated when he looked down to see Igul lying beneath him. The old man had opened his eyes at the same time as Ask and he looked up at his former apprentice with confusion.

The confusion disappeared almost immediately. Ask's moment of hesitation gave Igul enough time to strike. The old man's hand flicked up and fixed Bergr's wrist in a vice-like grip before the warrior had time to react. Pulling down, he easily forced the blade away from his throat and clamped his teeth down on the warrior's knuckles. Bergr howled in pain. The knife dropped from his injured hand.

Ask grabbed at Igul's face but the old houngan bucked his entire body, knocking Ask off-balance, then sat bolt upright. The top of Igul's head struck Bergr's chin and the warrior pitched over backwards, his jaw clacking shut with a sickening crack. The old houngan wrenched forward to slam his forehead into Ask's cheek. Ask's hands flew up too late to cover his face. A blossom of agony exploded across the side of his head, his vision suddenly clouded by tears of pain.

Hurt and off-balance, Ask offered little resistance as Igul grabbed his shoulder and shoved him bodily into the woman kneeling by his side. Ask's head slammed into Eydis' solar plexus and the two of them hit the snow in a tangle of limbs. Blinking the tears from his eyes, Ask scrambled off of Eydis and staggered upright, blinking tears from his eyes, trying to keep Igul in his sight.

Isond had snatched up Bergr's knife and risen to her feet. She held the weapon loosely in one hand as she faced off with Igul, trying to anticipate his movements. The possessed houngan moved like lightning, his speed and strength enhanced just as Hafgrim's had been. He pounced toward Isond, his fingers hooked like claws. She narrowly dodged with a quick step backwards, warding him off with a few quick, defensive swipes of the knife.

Ask pressed one hand to his cheek. He carefully probed with his fingers, ignoring the flashes of purple and red across his vision. The bone seemed intact, at the very least. He had no weapon. His spear had been lost at the cave and his knife was buried somewhere in the snow around Hafgrim's hut. Igul glanced toward him appraisingly, flicking his gaze between the young houngan and the woman with the knife.

Ask's mouth went dry. He didn't know if he could kill Igul. With Hafgrim, it had been different. He had known and respected the man, of course, but they had talked about it beforehand. He had had time to prepare himself mentally, harden his resolve. Igul had been right alongside him, as well, giving him the strength he needed to accept what they had to do. But Igul was his mentor. He'd lived with the old houngan, learning from him, for almost seven years. Hafgrim had been a friend, but Igul was family.

Igul's staff lay forgotten in the snow a dozen paces away. Ask had barely even started to move toward it when Igul lunged for him, one outstretched hand reaching for his face. Isond struck, her blade darting in to stab at the possessed houngan's side. He dodged narrowly, taking an awkward step sideways to evade the attack. She came after him, thrusting the knife toward him and forcing him onto the defensive. Ask used the distraction to dive toward Igul's fallen staff and scoop it from the snow.

He took the weapon firmly in both hands, brandishing it like a spear as he turned back toward the others. Isond had lost her slight advantage. Igul danced away from one of her knife thrusts and struck back, slapping the blade from her hand and stepping in to backhand her. She brought both of her arms up to shield her face but was still knocked backward by the force of the blow, falling hard on her rump.

Ask swung the staff and slammed it into the possessed houngan's temple, sending him stumbling to one side. Ask risked a quick glance to either side of him. Isond was already back on her feet, having recovered the knife that she had dropped into the snow. She circled around, trying to flank the possessed houngan.

Bergr, dazed by Igul's initial attack, had also managed to recover. His uninjured hand was held over his mouth, his fingers probing one cheek. Blood was smeared all over his face and dripped from his free hand where a strip of flesh had been torn away by the possessed houngan's teeth. Behind them, Eydis had managed to scramble up into a sitting position. The colour had drained from her features and one hand was clamped over the bandage wrapped around her thigh.

Igul turned to glower at Ask, flecks of dull golden light flashing in his eyes. He opened his mouth. Instead of words, a deep, buzzing drone spewed forth from his throat. Ask hesitated, caught off-guard. The sound seemed to take on a life of its own, filling the air around them. It was almost as though a cloud of insects were swarming around Hafgrim's hut—above, around and behind.

'What is it doing?' Isond hissed between clenched teeth, low enough that Ask almost didn't hear her. The droning was increasing in volume. 'What is it doing?'

'I am not sure!' said Ask.

Igul hadn't moved. The creature wearing his flesh simply stood there with his mouth open. Was it some sort of attack? The buzzing flowed around them, seemingly coming from every direction at once. Almost unconsciously, Ask glanced behind him and froze. A small child was just beyond the path that led to the hut, slowly walking toward them.

It was a boy, no more than a dozen winters old at the most, trudging toward them through the snow. His skin was pale, almost white. His eyes were dull and his mouth sagged open. He was a good thirty yards away, but it was immediately apparent to Ask that the sound was coming from his mouth as well. There was movement to either side. Ask flicked his gaze left and right, panic starting to rise in his chest. More children emerged from the trees. The closest was a girl of perhaps six winters, her long, platinum-blonde hair hanging loose around her gaunt features as she walked inexorably toward them.

'Bergdis...' Isond said, her voice a hoarse whisper. 'Domarsdottir.'

Trying to keep one eye on Igul, Ask turned slowly, marking off a quick tally in his head. There were almost two dozen. Ask's heart sank. They were surrounded. His mind went back to Engerdal, the houses filled with the weak and dying—no children to be seen in the entire village.

'What is wrong with them?' asked Isond. 'Is it controlling them?'

'I do not think so. Not directly,' Ask said. 'Look at their eyes.'

It was difficult to spot from this distance unless you were looking for it, but each of the children had small, dull flecks of golden light flickering through their eyes.

'What do we do?'

The buzzing ceased abruptly as the houngan and children closed their mouths seemingly simultaneously. 'Die,' spat Igul. 'You will die and feed us.'

'We cannot...I do not...' Ask said, his voice weak as he stumbled over his words.

Houngans and mambos were taught to show no mercy when fighting against the dark and malicious *monskellr* that haunted the Sundered Land. Put on the spot, however, Ask suddenly found his training difficult to reconcile with the opponents laid before him. Even when he had been forced to fight Igul, he had been upset and angry about the prospect of having to kill his old mentor; even then, he had tried not to hold back. But now, against this?

They were only children.

There had to be a way to save them. Ask shook himself—if they were being possessed by the same sort of creature that was in Igul, it was a moot point. The Innsmen were barely managing to survive against the one possessed houngan. Against a dozen opponents with the same sort of strength and speed? They would be torn to shreds, especially if Ask couldn't even bear to think about hurting them back.

Igul launched himself toward Ask with a buzzing shriek. Ask spun and managed to interpose his staff between himself and his attacker. The force of Igul's charge still knocked him from his feet. He landed hard on his back and an agonising, tearing pop heralded one set of stitches finally giving way. Igul lunged toward his face with an open mouth, trying to bite him. Ask managed to twist his staff, striking the possessed houngan in the side of the face. The hit knocked Igul off-balance and Ask pushed, using the opportunity to roll to one side and dump his opponent off of him.

At the same time, the children ran toward them, their hands twisted into claw-like shapes. Eydis raised her bow feebly, but did not release. Even with just a quick glance, Ask could tell that the children didn't seem to be moving any faster than they normally would have. The first pair reached Eydis and she batted at them with his bow. They grabbed at the weapon and she pulled it free, but a small girl latched onto her, burying fingers in her hair and biting at her face.

Bergr staggered forward to help, backhanding the girl child across the face with enough force to knock her from her feet. She clutched at her face with both hands, screaming and crying piteously and Bergr froze. Another three children took advantage of his sudden paralysis and swarmed him, grabbing and biting. In desperation, Bergr wrapped his forearm around a slightly older boy's throat and tried to use him as a shield, swinging the squirming child around to block the others.

Ask scrambled to one side, rising to his feet and bringing his staff around defensively in a single motion. Igul scarcely gave him a chance to recover, scuttling toward him on all fours. Before he had a chance to pounce, Isond was there. The possessed houngan tried to dodge to one side, but her knife sunk up to the hilt in his shoulder. He shrieked again and swung his arm, sweeping her feet from under her with a wild, backhanded blow.

The children reached them. Isond cried out as one grabbed her hair, pulling painfully. Another jumped on her chest, struggling to pin her to the ground. Ask went to help her, but Igul cut him off with one striding step, snarling. Bergdis Domarsdóttir shot past the possessed houngan and he followed, the small girl and old man lunging together toward Ask with outstretched hands.

Raising his hand in a defensive gesture, Ask gathered his power.

'*Lesir Hyrr bondye, pwoteje sèvitè ou kont sa ki mal sa a!*'

127

The barrier was wholly invisible this time, with not even a slight disturbance in the air to mark its presence. Ask's invocation was more focused, the energy given a solid form and shape rather than slopping out directionlessly as it had the first time he had created one.

Igul recoiled, managing to stop himself mid-leap as the barrier sprang into being between them. The child was not as lucky, charging headfirst into the energy. There was a sizzling snap at the point of impact and the girl bounced backward, a black, charred mark across her forehead. She landed hard on her backside and slumped into the snow, blinking dazedly.

The possessed houngan shied away, pausing momentarily to crouch down over the child, as though checking to see if she was okay. Ask dropped the barrier. It was a powerful defence, but it was too draining to use in an extended fight. He was already tired and hurt and could ill afford to waste his energy. Looking back up, Igul shot Ask a look of pure hatred and anger. The possessed houngan's right arm was hanging limp—Isond's knife must have severed something vital when she stabbed him.

Eydis let out a choking scream and Ask and Igul both glanced toward her. One of the young girls attacking her had sunk her teeth into the bloodied bandage wrapping her leg and torn it away. A shudder of pain rippled through Eydis' body as she flailed at her with one free arm. Her skin had turned ashen, the colour drained from her features.

'Ma!' Isond yelled, kicking desperately at her own attackers.

The children held on grimly, pinning her to the ground under the combined weight of their bodies. Igul smiled as he turned toward her, a humourless baring of teeth. Ask stepped forward as the possessed houngan moved, stabbing the end of his staff forward like a spear. The butt of the weapon caught Igul in the side, just below the ribcage. The old man stumbled.

Ask spun the staff in his hand, bringing the other end around to strike Igul across the chest as the possessed houngan twisted to defend himself. At the same time, Isond managed to get a hand across the face of one of the children and violently thrust him away from her. She got one foot under herself and sprang toward Igul, not waiting to catch her balance or brace herself properly. She grabbed at the knife still buried in the old man's shoulder and ripped it free. Already off-balance, Isond's charge was enough to send Igul sprawling to the snow.

'Back!' Ask stepped forward, lining up his staff as Isond rolled backwards off the old man.

He took a deep breath, focusing on the feel of the hard wood clenched in his fists. Thrusting the staff downward, he put his entire body weight behind the strike as he drove it into Igul's windpipe. There was a sickening crunching sound as the old man's throat was crushed. Igul's eyes opened impossibly wide. Isond rose to her feet next to Ask and was gone just as fast, her fists clenched as she descended upon the children attacking her mother.

Igul clawed at his throat helplessly, his jaw and tongue flapping as he tried to breathe or form words. His gold-flecked eyes locked on Ask. The same expression of utter hatred and malice as before twisted and distorted his features—a monstrous parody of someone Ask loved. Ask knelt down next to Igul, dropping the staff in the snow next to him and placed his hands on the old man's shoulders to stop him from rising again.

'Sssh, it's over.'

It felt as though his own throat had been crushed. Air entered his lungs in fits and starts as he resisted the tears welling in the corners of his eyes.

'It is over now. I am sorry. I was not strong enough,' he said. 'I am so sorry.'

The possessed houngan thrashed against him, grabbing at his arms desperately, but the enhanced strength the spirit had given the body was already abandoning it. Ask was left holding the shoulders of a dying old man, frantic to get up even as his body slowly shut down.

Tearing his tear-blurred vision away from Igul's dead, sightlessly staring eyes, Ask glanced toward Isond. At least three children lay unconscious, or perhaps dead, around where Eydis had fallen. Bergr still stood, struggling against the two squirming youths trapped in his arms. The remaining children had ceased their attack and were turning toward Ask, their eyes drawn to his hands. His mind didn't even register seeing them. All he saw was Isond, kneeling over her mother, her shoulders hunched in an unintentional mirror of Ask's own posture as she cried. Eydis wasn't moving.

Ask wracked his brain. He had no time to grieve yet. The *monskellr* was too powerful. Creating a spiritual barrier might buy a few seconds at most. Igul had tried to physically restraint it, but it had gnawed through his hand. The older houngan had started to summon heat—could the creature be incinerated? Even if it could, Ask would need to stop it from simply flying away.

Igul's struggles slowed, then ceased entirely. If Ask couldn't catch it in his hand…an idea occurred to him. It was a terrible, crazy idea with little chance of success, but it was still the best he could come up with.

130

'*Hyrr Jarl Virding, mwen bezwen dife ou. Hyrr Lorajaðr Virdingsson, boule lènmi m'. Se pou fòs kouraj ou ranpli m 'ak ban m' dife ou,*' Ask chanted, his voice broken and ragged. A lump began to visibly move up through Igul's crushed windpipe, forcing its way through the obstructed passageway. '*Boule ale monskellr sa a*…all of the Hyrr Lesir. Please, give me your fire.' Ask could feel the heat building. He'd done this countless times before, but never so hot, so quickly. The old man's body gave one final convulsion as the firefly burst free of his lips, springing into the air.

It shot toward his face and he flinched back, pressing his lips shut. There was a white flash of pain as the writhing, squirming creature tried to thrust itself into his mouth, biting at him with its powerful mandibles. If tears weren't already streaming down his cheeks, the pain would have been enough to summon them. A hiccoughing sob escaped his throat, and the *monskellr* shot inside.

Ask gagged as the thing started to force itself down his throat, couching and choking. He couldn't breathe. Even so, he maintained his focus on the power he had been gathering and increased its intensity as high as he could. The *monskellr* must have realised something was wrong. It stopped and started to wriggle back the way it had come.

Ask grimly clamped his jaw shut. The snow beneath him started to melt. The heat and fire he had created had collected deep inside his gullet. It did not burn him. He was a servant of Hyrr Lorajaðr Virdingsson, son of fire, and while he invoked his patron's name no flame could harm him. He forced the energy to rise, sending it up his throat to where the firefly creature was trapped inside his mouth.

The *monskellr* in his mouth was struggling frantically now. Around them, the children started to wail, an eerie

131

sound halfway between the normal grief of a child and the buzzing drone they had made earlier. They scrambled toward him, crying and screaming, but none made it to him. They dropped down into the snow one by one, writhing and shrieking, beating at their heads with their hands.

Ask could feel the creature biting and tearing at the inside of his mouth. The coppery tang of blood washed over his tongue, but he held firm. The thrashings of the *monskellr* started to wane. Ask waited until it had stilled completely before dismissing the power from his body. He relaxed his aching jaw and spat. A mouthful of blood and the blackened husk of what had been a firefly landed in the snow with a sizzling hiss.

Coughing and spluttering, he remained where he was for a few moments. He felt exhausted to his core and his throat and mouth stung where the creature had savaged him.

That effort had cost him more power than he had ever used before—even more than his first, unfocused attempt at a barrier invocation. He turned tired eyes toward Isond. She had not moved. He dropped his gaze to the children strewn between them. The youngsters were sobbing and crying still, but the oldest-looking one was already slowly pulling himself to his feet. His gold-flecked, red-rimmed eyes fixed Ask with a look of pure hate and anger.

Forcing himself to move, Ask stood and started toward the youth. He closed the gap between them with four quick strides. The boy raised his hands to grab at him, a snarl twisting his features. Without pause or hesitation, Ask lashed out with his fist, catching the boy square in the jaw. The snarl turned to a surprised yelp of pain as he toppled backward into the snow, stunned. Ask continued past him, carefully avoiding the weakly grasping hands of the other children as he came to Isond's side.

'Bergr.' Despite the way Ask felt, his voice seemed oddly calm and in control. He spat another mouthful of blood into the snow.

Bergr looked over to meet his gaze. A flicker of acknowledgement passed between them. The warrior moved toward him without a word, the children he had been wrestling with already dropped to the snow.

'Go to Fulnir. See if you can wake him,' said Ask.

Taking Isond roughly by the shoulder, Ask pulled her away from her dead or dying mother. There was no resistance. She simply moved as he directed, rising to her feet with a stumble. He steered her toward where Fulnir still lay unconscious in the snow near the destroyed wall of Hafgrim's hut. He felt a slight tightening in his chest. There was little chance that Isond would be so easily removed from her mother's side if was still possible to save her. Eydis was already dead, then.

It was his fault. If Ask had been stronger, or faster, Eydis would not be lying on the ground, her lifesblood staining the snow bright red. He steeled himself. There was no time to dwell on that. They were still outnumbered and surrounded by stunned, but recovering, enemies. He needed to make a decision. Quickly.

While the children were disoriented, they were vulnerable. They didn't seem to have the same sort of enhanced strength as Igul or Hafgrim. If he didn't do something quickly, they would recover their wits and he wasn't sure that the three of them could handle another combined attack. Part of him pointed out that it would be a trivial matter at this stage to simply go from child to child and put them out of their misery. Quietly, he told that part of himself to leap off a cliff. He wasn't going to save the Engermen by murdering their children. Eydis and Igul had already joined the others that had lost their lives fighting against this evil. It felt as though Ask might lose his mind if he saw any more death today.

'He is still out,' Bergr said. The warrior had gone to Fulnir's side, as instructed. 'It looks bad.'

Ask already knew it was bad. He had seen the ugly blue and purple mottling over Fulnir's face when he had tried to wake him earlier. He would be no help to them. Ask looked back at the disoriented, stumbling children. Something fell into place in his mind. Saying nothing, he bent over to retrieve the staff from where it lay next to Igul's body. He thrust the end of the staff into the snow and limped around the children in a wide arc, dragging the tip as he went.

It had puzzled him at first. He had guessed that perhaps the creature had been merely controlling the children and that once it was killed they would revert back to normal. After he had incinerated the firefly, however, the children were still behaving the same way. Their eyes were flecked with gold light just as Hafgrim and Igul's had been. They were clearly possessed by the same sort of creatures, but if that were the case, then why weren't they as strong as the other had been? Why were they possessing mere children instead of grown men?

Bergdis, the young girl with the white-blonde hair, grabbed at his leg as he passed her. Ask raised his foot, placed it firmly against her shoulder and kicked hard. She sprawled backwards, tumbling into another child. They collapsed in a heap in the snow as Ask continued to circle around them. Others reached for him, but he quickened his pace to evade them. He would have been jogging if not for his injured knee.

It only made sense if creatures were weaker than the one Ask had killed. They had only come out of hiding once Igul was possessed and the rest of the Innsmen injured. Ask completed his circuit, rejoining Isond and Bergr where they stood silently. Several children had risen to their feet and were stumbling toward them. Ignoring them, Ask lowered himself gingerly into the snow to sit cross-legged at the edge of the circle he had drawn.

'Houngan?' Bergr's voice quavered.

Ask ignored him as well. His attention was entirely absorbed by what he was about to do. The pattern of energy was already locked in his mind, but he was changing it, tweaking the design to suit a different purpose than originally intended.

'*Kald Jarl Løgur, mwen bezwen bon konprann ou. Vatn Jarl Dauðvís, mèt nan passerelles, defann chemen sa a. Se pou pa gen yon sèl pase.*'

A boy of seven or eight winters lunged at him, stumbling over his own feet. Ask did not flinch. Instead, the child bounced off the air in front of him, letting out a buzzing yelp of pain as he fell. There was not so much as a ripple in the air to mark the barrier's presence, this time.

Ask sat motionless, his mind fixated on discovering the best way to use the least amount of power to maintain the magic while still giving his barrier the strength it needed to contain the creatures.

Time passed slowly. The trapped children tried unsuccessfully to escape the trap that contained them. At first they simply threw themselves at Ask, vainly attempting to reach the houngan or break his concentration. After a while, they started getting more desperate, clawing at the sides of the circle, heedless of the energy that nipped at their flesh. Some started crying again.

'Ask...?'

He hadn't heard Isond approach him. If he let himself be too distracted it would take more energy to maintain the barrier. He had no idea how long he was going to have to keep it up for. The barrier was only a delaying tactic. Ask trusted Isond to look after Fulnir, and when Fulnir woke up he'd have time to think up a solution.

Fulnir would put together a ritual to force the creatures from the children or come up with some other way to save them. Ask didn't let himself think too long on the questions that immediately popped into his mind: What if Fulnir didn't wake up? What if he did wake up, but couldn't figure out a way to save the children? Others would be on their way to help them, but it would likely be days before even Mam Botvi or Mam Sida from Billingstad, the next-nearest village beyond Innset, turned up. Sustaining an active barrier like this would be draining, even if he only had to keep it going for a few hours. Ask didn't know how long he could keep it up.

A hand tentatively touched his shoulder. 'Let me help,' Isond said.

The trickle of power that she channelled into him wasn't much, but it helped. 'It was nesting, I think,' he murmured.

'What?'

'The creature that possessed Hafgrim. I do not know what it is, but it was nesting. We caught it not long after it had reproduced.' His voice was quiet, and he felt like he was

136

talking from very far away. 'It was keeping the Engermen alive as a source of food. It took their children to keep as hosts for its young. They are immature, not yet fully grown into their power. It is why I am able to trap them. I could not have held Hafgrim or Igul like this.'

Isond didn't respond. Ask wasn't sure if it was because she was concentrating or because she had nothing left to say. Either way, he was grateful enough to her for simply being there.

- - -

Ask couldn't see. Some part of him knew his eyes were open, but any effort expended on processing what they were seeing was a waste of energy that he desperately needed to power the barrier. His insides gnawed at him and he vaguely tried to remember how long ago it had been since he'd eaten. The night before their attack on Hafgrim. How long ago was that, now? He had no idea. He'd lost track of the time he'd spent sitting here.

Ask felt hollow. Used up. His senses were dulled, even discounting the fact that he dared not use any of his energy to focus on what they were telling him. He had not slept. He had enough awareness to realise it had gotten dark at some point, and light again, then dark, then light…how many days had it been? Two? Three? More? Had it even been a day, or was his mind playing tricks on him? He didn't know. It had hurt for a while, once he had to strain himself to sustain the magic. The pain had been absorbed by the aches and complaints of the rest of his body, the whole turning into a sort of dull roar of agony that he pushed to the back of his mind. It was distracting. He couldn't afford distractions.

At least someone had thought to try to get him to drink. He hadn't said anything. It would have used up precious energy. It had been all he could to let his mouth open as they poked his lips with the gourd, and swallow to stop himself from choking on the water when they had poured it down his throat.

Occasionally a hand was placed on Ask's back to supply him with more energy. The weaker trickle was Isond, of course, but Fulnir must have awakened at some point. They were taking turns helping ease Ask's burden. While Fulnir poured strength into him, Ask could use the other man's power to maintain the barrier while he let his own recover for a time. When Fulnir stopped, Isond would take over. She didn't have the energy to sustain the invocation herself, but the steady dribble of strength was enough to at least ease the strain on him. Isond, Fulnir. Isond, Fulnir. Over and over.

Part of him thought about simply giving up. Dropping the barrier, letting the children out. At some point they had stopped testing their prison. They would be hungry, too. How long could the creatures survive with no blood to feed on but that of their host? How long could the children go without food? Ask didn't know. The point of trapping them wasn't to make them starve to death. He'd only wanted to buy time until Fulnir woke up and had time to think of a way to save them. Instead, Fulnir and Isond were still taking turns helping sustain the barrier.

Ask didn't look at them. He dared not distract himself, even enough to make sure his eyes still, in fact, worked. It was entirely possible he had gone blind. The strain he was placing on his body by maintaining the magic for days might have forced his body to start sacrificing parts of itself to continue on.

The hand on his shoulder disappeared. The trickle of energy it had been channelling to him vanished. Through the dull haze, Ask felt a twinge of puzzlement. It was true that he had lost track of time, but it didn't feel like it had been that long since Fulnir and Isond had last switched over. There was a noise. Some part of Ask realised that someone was trying to talk to him, but he couldn't make out the words.

A pair of strong hands took hold of his shoulders and pulled him gently backwards. The unexpected feeling of being pulled off-balance was enough to disrupt his concentration. His mind fumbled awkwardly as it tried to compensate. He tried to mumble some words, tell whoever it was to stop—he needed to maintain the magic or the children would escape. Uncrossing his legs, he attempted to put his feet on the ground and stand up in protest. One hand reached out to grope blindly for the edge of the barrier.

A firm pressure gripped his wrist and drew it back toward his body as the hands at his shoulders steadied him. Had they not, there would have been nothing stopping him from collapsing to the ground. Instead, he found himself being laid gently onto the cold snow. The barrier slipped from his mind. His physical connection to the magic broke and Ask felt a shuddering spasm run through the length of his body. It felt as if a massive weight had just been lifted from him. The relief after the long build-up of pressure was like a physical blow. All of his wounds clamoured to be heard, crying out in protest against the sudden reinstatement of feeling in his nerves.

He felt sick. Suddenly he couldn't breathe and it was only with a dim sort of clarity that he realised it was because he was too busy retching. The taste of bile filled his mouth. Hacking and spitting feebly, he tried to form words again, but his mouth only seemed capable of making small, meaningless noises instead. His tongue was thick in his mouth, the inside of his throat raw and painful.

The coldness surrounding him huddled close, hugging him tightly in a frozen embrace. He fell into it, letting it wash over him as his thoughts faded into darkness.

- - -

A dull roar of pain through Ask's entire body greeted him as he slowly drifted back into consciousness. His muscles ached as they recalled how he had treated them. His head felt as though it were stuffed with wool. Opening his eyes slowly, he blinked away the crusty mucus gluing his eyelids closed. Blotches of pallid colour clouded his vision, blurry and indistinct. The pain in his arm sharpened as he tried to reach up to wipe at his eyes, the limb barely even shifting from its resting place. His lips parted and he let out a barely-audible groan.

'Houngan? Are you awake?' A familiar voice was at his side. Male.

Ask tried to blink harder in an attempt to clear his vision as he tilted his head toward the source. A jolt of pain shot down his neck at the movement and he winced. Summoning his scattered and unfocused will he forced open his mouth to try to speak. 'Who are you? Where am I?' His swollen tongue twitching dryly in his mouth as he managed something that may have been recognisable as speech.

'Easy, houngan. Easy. You need to rest still.'

There was a pause and a sound like someone rummaging about. Ask felt a hand carefully slide under his head to tilt it forward. A black shape loomed in his vision as a gourd was pressed to his lips. Water dribbled into his mouth.

'Here. Drink,' the voice instructed.

Ask did as he was told. The cold water stung the lacerations in his mouth, where the firefly had torn into him, but he ignored it. The pain helped to bring him more solidly into the realm of consciousness. Greedily sucking at the trickle of liquid, Ask finally noticed what his other senses were telling him over the white noise of the pain that seemed to coat every nerve in his body. It didn't feel as though he was wearing any clothes, though there was a tightness around his chest and back that he recognised as bandages. There was a similar binding around his injured knee, preventing it from moving. He was lying on and under something warm and soft. Furs.

After a few seconds of drinking, Ask's throat seized up. He coughed and spluttered, his aching muscles strongly protesting the sudden movement by sending another wave of angry pain shooting through his body. The gourd was removed from his lips and a gentle hand was placed on his chest instead.

'Careful, houngan. Are you okay?'

Ask finally recognised the voice. Bergr. He rested a second, focusing on his breathing as he recovered from the coughing fit. The hands withdrew from Ask's chest and behind his head. After a few moments he tilted his head to the side again, ignoring the protests of his neck. His vision swam lazily back into focus as he tried to concentrate on the blurred silhouette next to him. Bergr remained silent. After what felt like hours had passed, Ask felt strong enough to try to talk again. 'What...happened? Wh-where?'

'It is okay. You are in Engerdal. Almersson's home.'

'Almersson?' Ask grasped at his memories, the recollections slipping from his mind like water between fingers. 'The children? Where are they? What happened?'

'I...Mam Botvi said that you might have some trouble remembering.'

'Botvi? Mam Botvi is here?'

Bergr nodded. 'Her and Mam Sida both.'

'How long have I been...?'

'Three days, more or less,' Bergr said, his tone uncertain. 'When the mambos got here they took you off of the circle and you passed out. After they took care of the children, we brought you back here with everyone else.'

'I have been unconscious for three days?' The length of time he had been out for seemed almost surreal. Ask pushed further questions about that to the side as he found his mind fixating on something else the other man had said. 'What happened to the children?'

'They are safe, for the most part. It was a good thing you did, houngan, holding them like that. Mam Sida was able to drive out the dark spirits that were inside them. Isond told the mambos how you cooked the one that took Houngan Hafgrim and Houngan Igul and we built a bonfire to burn the others in once they were out of the children.'

'Good. Good.' Ask felt himself relax. He hadn't noticed how tense his body had suddenly become when he had asked after the children.

Bergr hesitated for a moment before continuing. 'One child is still missing. Dagr's boy. He is seven.'

'Kerling's teats,' Ask swore, his body tense once again. One had gone missing? That could mean that one of the firefly creatures had escaped. 'Innset?'

'They know. If he headed that way, he will be found.'

'With a three day head start…has anyone been sent out? Trackers?'

'A six day head start. It has been three days since the others got here, but before that we spent another three waiting for them.'

Ask didn't respond straight away. Three days maintaining the barrier. That sort of constant drain over that long a time was dangerous. It could have even been lethal. His memories were still foggy, but he could recall now some of the exhaustion he had felt. He had lost track of time, focused on the task of keeping the children contained. It could have killed him if Mam Botvi and Mam Sida had taken any longer to arrive than they had. No wonder he'd been out for so long afterward—he hadn't just passed out, he'd been in a coma.

His eyes having finally adjusted to the point where he could see reasonably well, Ask glanced past Bergr. The home was one of the familiar low-set dug-ins with a small fire pit in the middle and a single exit. The lone door stood open, a cool breeze filtering in from outside. From where he lay, Ask could see only the clear blue of the sky and the snow-covered roof of another structure through the door. Subdued sounds drifted in from outside; voices talking, footsteps crunching in the snow and other signs of activity.

'Mam Botvi told me to come and get her once you woke up,' Bergr said. Despite his words, he didn't move from Ask's side.

Ask looked back at him. The warrior's face was bruised, dark purple and blue splashed across his squashed nose and marked the areas underneath his eyes.

'No. I will go myself in a moment,' Ask said.

Bergr's forehead creased in concern. 'I do not think you are well enough to walk yet. Meaning no disrespect, houngan.'

'I will be soon. Just…wait a few minutes before you go running off to Mam Botvi. Give me a little time.'

'I…yes. As you say, houngan.' Bergr fell silent.

Ask lay back and closed his eyes as his body relaxed. He took a deep breath and started to perform some of the mental exercises he had learnt during his training to try to focus himself. Ignoring the pains and aches of his body was hard, but he had to pack it all away so that he could function. His body was weak from lack of food, but the thought of eating something right away turned his stomach. Once he'd had a chance to centre himself and stretch his muscles, then he would see about replenishing his body's energy reserves.

A short time later, Ask's eyes flicked open again. Taking another deep breath in preparation, he carefully started to pull himself up. His muscles rebelled against the movement. He could feel his arms trembling from the effort as he managed to get himself in a sitting position.

Next to him, Bergr rose and offered his hand. Ask took it gratefully, trying to keep his hand steady to hide his difficulty. As he struggled to his feet, however, his legs gave out and he stumbled to his knees. Bergr was ready for it, stooping down and slipping Ask's arm around his shoulders for support. Ask leaned heavily on him, tears springing to the corners of his eyes. His injured knee burned like fire when he had tried to put weight on it. It was all he could do to keep from crying out.

'Houngan...'

'I am fine,' Ask said, his chest juddering with strained breaths. 'Hold a moment.'

They stood silently for a few moments while Ask recovered himself again. Once he felt confident he was well enough, Bergr helped him to dress in a loose-fitting cotton tunic and wrapped a fur cloak around his shoulders. The warrior left him leaning up against the side of the doorway while he recovered Igul's staff and handed it to him to use as a walking stick. Ask paused a moment, the hard wood familiar beneath his fingers, letting himself remember.

Igul was dead. It had been three days since Mam Botvi and Mam Sida had arrived, according to Bergr, so they would have already performed the funeral rites. Ask had missed out on his only real chance to say goodbye to the old man. Of course, he could always invoke the houngan's spirit and ask it to watch over him, but talking to a disembodied presence wouldn't be the same. Ask thought about the vision he had been given by Jarl Løgur during his initiation. Igul had said that he had had a vision of his own death, as well. Had he known how close it had been?

Holding the staff tight and close to his body, Ask leant his weight onto it and shuffled slowly out the door. The bright light made his eyes water and he blinked rapidly until they adjusted. Bergr fell into step beside him, ready to intercede if it looked like he needed any more help.

The faint smell of cooked fish reached Ask's nose and he followed it, pointedly ignoring the distress signals coming from his stomach. People were scattered amongst the dug-in houses of Engerdal, mostly gathered around outside fires or trudging wearily from one place to another. Even so, people Ask had seen on the brink of death a week ago were up and about, seemingly well on their way to their old selves.

Ask noticed several Innsmen, their healthy colour and strong, sure movements starkly contrasted against the recovering Engermen. Some called out greetings as the two men slowly made their way past. Ask acknowledged them with a forced smile and dip of his head. His attention was caught momentarily by the sight of a young boy, perhaps twelve winters old, helping his mother carry furs and woven blankets. The child had an ugly purple bruise painted across his jawline. Ask winced guiltily and looked away.

They came across the mambos with two of their hounsis by a cook fire that had burned down to glowing coals. Several other people were gathered nearby, one child finishing off the last of the meal they had just shared. They all watched quietly as Ask approached.

Those not houngan, mambo or apprentice left at a word from Mam Sida. Bergr waited until Ask carefully lowered himself down to sit on a log next to the fire, then inclined his head respectfully toward the mambos and left as silently as he had come.

'Foolish man,' said Botvi to Ask, shaking her head. Botvi was young. She had been made mambo not long after Ask started his own apprenticeship, and he could still remember her raising. 'Just as headstrong as Igul was. You still need rest.'

'I have rested enough for now,' Ask said.

'As you say.' The corners of Sida's mouth quirked upward in a smile, wrinkling her tattoo. It was an odd design, more flowing and elegant than most. Grace and charm—Ask had heard that Sida had been quite the beauty in her own youth. 'It is good to see you on your feet, regardless.'

Aldis and Fastvi, the mambos' hounsis', sat quietly while their elders spoke. Ask wondered whether or not the third, Fjotra, was about the village somewhere as well or if she had remained in Billingstad. 'Fulnir told you what happened here?'

Botvi nodded. 'I only heard of a creature like that once before, many years ago now. Adze, they are called. Powerful, dangerous things. Rare enough I had near forgotten they existed. It was only by luck and the blessing of the Lesir that you happened across the best way to kill one.'

'Adze.' Ask turned the word over in his mouth. Igul had never mentioned them before, Ask was sure. It was possible that he hadn't known of their existence at all. 'They can control other *monskellr*? Use blood magic?'

'Maybe, though I never heard anything about that,' Botvi said with a frown. 'Fulnir told us about the tokoloshe as well. Very strange to have so many *monskellr* gathering in such a small area without a bokor controlling them. But it was already using the blood of the Engermen, though, to feed its young. It does not make much sense that it would be using blood magic as well.'

'But the tokoloshe protected it.'

'I know. Fulnir said it was like they were guarding them, the adze and its offspring.'

Sida poked at the coals with a stick. '*Monskellr* working together like that…it is troubling,' she said.

A morose silence fell. No one seemed to want to bring up Hafgrim or Igul. Part of Ask was glad for that. He wasn't sure he could handle talking about them just yet. They would have plenty of time to talk about them later, once he had had a chance to let everything sink in.

'Ask.'

He looked over his shoulder, surprised to see Fulnir and Isond there. Lost in his own thoughts, he hadn't even heard them approach.

'Good to see you awake,' Fulnir said. A smile curved his lips, but did not touch his eyes.

'It is good to see you as well.' Ask looked back at the others around the fire. 'We will talk more later.'

There was a murmur of agreement in response. Ask planted the butt of his staff firmly on the ground and used it to carefully pull himself to his feet. Fulnir looked as though he was about to move to help, but Ask raised a hand to wave him off. Once he had struggled back to his feet, the three of them slowly walked away from the fire.

Ask suppressed a wince every time he limped on his injured leg, but they continued on until they had gotten far enough away from any other people that he judged they would not be absently overheard. There was a small birch tree nearby and he hobbled over to it, resting his back against the trunk and sliding down to sit at its base. He flicked his cloak underneath his rump to offer some measure of protection from the cold snow. Isond and Fulnir dropped down next to him, forming a rough circle.

Fulnir had rested his chin in his hands. 'I wish there was something we could have done,' he said quietly.

Ask shook his head. 'There was not. Once a spirit fully takes control of your body, the only way to get rid of it is to have it leave of its own volition. That is why the Lesir only mount those who give themselves willingly.'

148

'Could you have captured Hafgrim, as you did the children?' Fulnir persisted, though his tone was half-hearted. He already knew what Ask was going to say. 'We could have worked out a way to force it out, somehow.'

Beside him, Isond reached out to touch his shoulder reassuringly.

'I was barely strong enough to keep the children contained, and they were much weaker than their parent. It broke through Igul's barrier like it was not even there. There was no way any of us could have contained it, not without help and preparation.'

Fulnir sighed. 'I know. Just…Igul.'

'I know,' Ask said.

'I can scarcely believe they are dead.'

'We will manage. There is still so much that needs to be done.' Ask paused, considering his words before speaking again. 'You should know I am going to tell Sida that I think you are ready to be a houngan. Not to ask for permission, but for her help with the ceremonies. I have not raised someone before.'

Fulnir didn't even look up at Ask. The statement hung in the air, waiting for the other man to react in some way. Long seconds dragged by before Fulnir gave a despairing chuckle and shook his head, covering his face with one hand. 'I do not even care. I always thought I would be so happy, when I was to become houngan.'

'We have all been through a lot,' Ask said gently.

'Seven years. Seven years training to be a houngan. I wanted it so badly. But not like this.'

'I know. But with Igul and Hafgrim gone, I am going to need help looking after Innset and Engerdal.'

'You will stay?'

Fulnir knew that Ask had planned to go travelling across the Sundered Land once he had become a houngan, much as Igul had done in his youth. 'Of course I will stay,' Ask said, reaching out to place a hand on his friend's shoulder. 'I cannot leave now. Maybe in a few years, once people are settled and everything is back to normal. Right now, my responsibility is to Innset and Engerdal.'

'Thank you. I—'

'Do not thank me just yet,' Ask said, a ghost of a smile crossing his features. 'I have been a houngan for half a month now and believe me when I say it is nowhere near as much fun as we thought it would be.'

They fell silent again, simply sitting quietly in each other's company. Ask let his eyes wander back toward the subdued activity of the village. Less than a stone's throw away, he could see Luta and her daughter, Bergdis. Luta was grinding something using a mortar and pestle, the stone bowl resting on the ground in front of her as she leant over it. Her daughter sat nearby, playing with a small woven doll of some kind. Ask could see her lips moving as she made the toy dance in front of her. For a moment his mind recalled the child as she had been while possessed—a white-blonde wight stalking toward them, her mouth open as the buzzing drone filled the air. He blinked, dismissing the image, and turned back to Isond and Fulnir.

'We should go help.' Fulnir broke the silence, scratching at his neck. 'There is still much to be done.'

Isond nodded agreement. Ask inclined his head as well. 'I will stay here for a bit longer,' he said.

Fulnir looked at him. 'You will rest. You damn near killed yourself back there. I know you. Do not overdo it before you have had a proper chance to recover. Have you even eaten anything yet?'

A small smile touch Ask's lips. His stomach had settled now and had been demanding his attention for some time. 'I will find something soon. You worry too much.'

Fulnir rose to his feet, Isond joining him a moment later. 'I will be watching,' he said. 'You will get your rest even if I have to put you to bed myself.'

Ask gave a small chuckle as his friend started to leave. 'Isond, will you hold a moment?' he asked. 'There is something I want to talk to you about.'

Isond stopped, smiling at Fulnir and raising her hand in a small wave of farewell. He smiled back, though to Ask's eye the expression seemed forced, then turned and started back toward the village's centre. The two of them watched him leave. After a moment or two, Isond glanced back down toward Ask and tilted her head to one side.

'I just wanted to thank you,' he said, letting the words stand on their own for a moment.

'For what?'

'Everything.' Ask dug his staff into the ground and used it to lever himself up into a standing position, so he could look her eye-to-eye. 'You were the one who pestered me to go after Fulnir and Igul when I was hesitating. When we found the Engermen, you were right there doing everything you could to help. The talk we had at Domar's farm? It was…' He paused for a second to consider his words. 'I needed it. We would not have done half as well against the tokoloshe or that thing that was controlling Hafgrim if you had not been here. I had forgotten how capable you are.'

Isond smiled and looked away, a touch of colour rising to her cheeks. 'I…Well. You are welcome, houngan.'

'And I am sorry about your mother,' Ask said quietly. Isond's smile vanished. 'I did not know what we were fighting. If I had been quicker. If it had not—'

'Stop,' she said. Her tone had a slight edge to it, and he noticed that her hands had balled into fists. She was quiet for a few moments and Ask did not dare continue. 'You were trying to save Houngan Igul. You were trying to save everyone. You did not know there was more than one. You did not do anything wrong.'

'But if I had been thinking clearly, or if—'

'I said *stop*,' Isond interrupted again, this time turning back to glare at him. There was anger in her eyes. For a moment, Ask thought she might strike him. 'Your 'if's do not matter. My mother knew how dangerous it would be. She accepted that and came anyway, when she could have hung back and let us take care of it ourselves. She was a warrior, not some girl child you were looking after.'

'I…that is not what I meant, I was just…' Ask searched for the words. 'I am sorry. I wish things had gone differently. That is all.'

Isond took a deep breath, exhaling too sharply for it to be called a sigh. There was a moment of silence before she spoke again, her voice still hard. 'So do I, but passing out blame is not useful right now. There is still so much to be done.'

Ask nodded. 'We should go and see what we can do to help.'

Isond shook her head and gave a small snort of derision. '*I* will go and see what I can do to help. *You* need to get something into your stomach and get some more rest.

You are one of the ones that need help right now and you are going to act like it even if Fulnir and I need to sit on you to keep you bedridden.'

'As you say,' he said, a smile touching his lips. He raised his free hand in a placating gesture. 'There will be no need for that. I will go.'

The two of them walked back into the village, Isond slowing her pace to match Ask's hobbling gait. Ask knew that Isond and Fulnir were right. If he pushed himself too hard before his body and spirit had had a chance to recover, he might do himself some permanent harm. Even so, after he'd eaten something he had no intention of going back to sleep. He'd been sleeping for three days—how could he go back to bed while there was still so much that needed to be done?

- - -

The child trudged wearily through the forest. He was barely able to summon the strength to struggle through the snow lying thickly on the ground. His legs were starting to refuse his instructions, the nerves in them deadened by the unrelenting cold. A light but icy breeze tugged at his clothes and hair, dusting his body with flakes of fresh white as they tumbled from the sky. He was shivering almost uncontrollably, but he didn't know how to start a fire or anything else that might have kept him warm.

Flecks of congealed, frozen blood were splattered across his hands. He had managed to feed on one of the Engermen before fleeing the village, and had caught a snow fox a day or so ago. Their blood had brought him this far, but he would need more soon or he would starve. His last meal seemed so long ago, an eternity between the him of then and the him of now.

A silhouette glided between the trees, stark black contrasted against the white snow and birch trees. Something stalking him? The child stopped in his tracks, blinking to clear the frozen tears from his blurred vision. The presence was felt as well as seen—a dark, malevolent force that the child was surprised he hadn't felt earlier as it approached. Panic rose in his chest, but he pushed it away and drew himself up defiantly.

The figure resolved into a tall man, a formless blackness enveloping his body. He seemed completely untouched by the wind, his long, dark hair lying loose and undisturbed. The falling snow passed through his pale flesh as though he were not truly there. Looking down at the child, he smiled a wide, mirthless grin. As his lips peeled back, the child could see that his mouth was filled with thin, needle-like fangs, each the length of a finger.

Suddenly, the man crouched, hunkering down to the child's eye-level. One thin white hand reached out, its fingers tipped with long, claw-like nails. The child flinched slightly as it rested gently on his head. 'Be at ease child. There is no need to fear me,' he said. His voice was surprisingly ordinary. 'Your mother was my ally. I am sorry I did not come swiftly enough to save her.'

The note of regret in the man's tone seemed genuine. Feeling his shoulders sag, the child bit his lip and tasted the coppery tang of his blood. He had cried when his mother had been killed. He would not cry again, not in front of this man.

'I will need to you tell me exactly what happened,' the man said. He looked down at the child and shook his head.

'Not yet. Look at you, half-starved. Come, we will hunt and then we will rest. We can speak later. For now, I will watch over you. You will be safe.'

The amorphous blackness covering the man's body warped and extended, draping itself around the child like a hooded cloak and swallowing him up completely. A moment later, they were both gone. The falling snow covered the child's trail, until it was as if no one had been there at all.

TALES OF THE SUNDERED LAND
The Flame's Burden

- - -

Matthew Karabache is addicted to stories of all kinds, devouring those made up by others and creating his own with equal gusto. Mythology and folklore hold a special fascination for him and he plunders them for ideas and other riches like some sort of literary pirate. He has been writing for as long as he can remember and will continue to do so for ever and ever. You can't stop him, so there. He lives in Brisbane, Australia.

www.ingramcontent.com/pod-product-compliance
Lightning Source LLC
Chambersburg PA
CBHW021055130626
46552CB00005B/2115